THE CLARKS OF WILLSBOROUGH POINT

THE LONG TREK NORTH

Darcey Hale

TBR Books
Brooklyn, New York

TBR Books
146 Norman Avenue
Brooklyn, New York

For a listing of books published by TBR Books, visit our website at www.tbr-books.com or contact us by email at: contact@tbr-books.com

Front Cover Illustration: Willsboro Point © Philip Hall
Back Cover Portrait: Darcey Hale © Nancie Battaglia
Cover Design © Nathalie Charles

ISBN 978-1-947626-12-6 (paperback)
ISBN 978-1-947626-13-3 (eBook)

Library of Congress Control Number: 2018951082

DEDICATION

It is with sincere gratitude that I dedicate this, my first book, to those who have stayed with me through thick and thin. Without their encouragement and support I would never have had the courage to undertake such an endeavor in my eighty-fourth year.

Thank you, Morris, for being such a good friend and mentor, and for your wise guidance as I learned to work with the Clark Collection in a respectful and professional manner.

Thank you, son, Philip for your tireless willingness to pick up the pieces as I drowned over and over dealing with the vicissitudes of a computer, and for your beautiful cover photograph.

Thank you, Ron, our Town Historian, for so willingly sharing your vast knowledge of the history of Willsboro and guiding me to the resources that I have needed.

Thank you, a thousand times over, Fabrice, for having such faith that I could actually write a book and then spending endless hours editing and publishing it.

And, finally, I owe a huge vote of appreciation for the unending patience of my husband, Bruce, who has given me the time and support I needed in order to bring my story to life.

ACKNOWLEDGMENTS

I wish to acknowledge the many individuals and organizations that have played such an important role in celebrating the importance of the Clark Collection, as it represents the Clarks of Willsboro Point and their landholdings, and now by beginning to tell their story through this book and those to follow.

Each member of the Hale Historical Research Foundation Board so generously shared their skills and expertise, as well as their professional support, as we sought a permanent home for the Clark Collection. Many thanks to Joe Burke, Art Cohn, Jim Fuller, Cory Gillilland, Morris Glenn, Bruce Hale, Nick Muller, Patty Paine, Teresa Sayward, Lorilee Sheehan, and Caroline Welsh. You have accomplished your goal!

Several New York State professionals have been of great assistance in a variety of ways. Thank you, Bernie Margolis (New York State Librarian until his untimely death) for your enthusiastic support of what I have done and your eagerness to make the Clark Collection a part of the greater State Library Collection. Thank you, Peter Nastasi, New York State Library, Manuscripts and Special Collections, for your commitment to ensuring that the Clark Collection will always be cared for and will be accessible to a wide audience in the future. Thank you, Bill Krattinger, of the New York State Historic Preservation Office, for seeing that the former Clark property is listed on the National Register of Historic Places as the Ligonier Point Historic District. Thank you Connie Frisbee Houde, New York State Museum, for sharing your knowledge of textiles and clothing with me as we sifted through 2,100 of them.

Thank you, Hallie Bond for bearing with me as I have tried to learn about quilts and quilting, as well as Jane Mackintosh and Ted Comstock who taught us so much during the month-long appraisal of the paper portion of the Clark Collection.

Thank you, Teresa Sayward, formerly our State Assemblywoman and Town Supervisor, and Shaun Gilliland, our Town Supervisor, for your support and encouragement in all regards. Finally, thank you Linda Hacker, Rinda Foster and those others who have read my story and encouraged me to keep going.

TABLE OF CONTENTS

An Invitation _____ 1

The Scene Is Set _____ 7

Lives Intertwined _____ 13

Preparations For The Journey _____ 21

The Long Trek North _____ 27

Lake Champlain At Last_____ 41

Journey's End_____ 45

A New Life Begins_____ 53

The Anchor Shop_____ 65

Willsborough Is Home _____ 73

Happy Years For George And Lydia_____ 81

Good Years For All _____ 91

The Community's Embrace In Tragedy _____ 99

References_____ 107

Notes_____ 111

Index _____ 119

About The Author _____ 125

Hale Historical Research Foundation _____ 127

AN INVITATION

Sometimes destiny and fate land one in the most unexpected places, places that hold untold treasures and unknown opportunities. This is just what happened one day in 1996, when my husband, Bruce, first introduced me to Willsboro, New York - a small, rural town on the western shore of Lake Champlain that is packed full of history. We drove through the Village, over the bridge that spans the Boquet River, up the steep hill that leads one out of the river valley, and on north to Willsboro Point. Before long, we turned east onto Ligonier Point, a thumb of land stretching out into the lake, where we started down a quiet country lane lined with stately 150-year-old sugar maple trees that arched their gnarled limbs overhead. When we made our way toward the lake I had no idea that I would soon be embarking upon an amazing journey into the past - a journey that would change my life forever.

As we continued down Ligonier Way, a complex of nineteenth century family homes and outbuildings that Orrin Clark and his descendants had created to support their lives as farmers, quarrymen and boat builders came within our view. Bruce explained that by the end of the century the once thriving community they had created began to slowly wither away. Buildings that no longer had a purpose were torn down, or simply left to fall to the earth as their timbers rotted away. The property began to assume a seasonal nature and the houses only came to life during the warm summer months. As the days grew shorter, and the first whispers of the coming of Autumn were heard, windows were shuttered, and doors were closed once again. Ligonier Point and its yet unknown treasures lapsed back into silent darkness, hidden from view, lost from the human mind, except for brief moments of activity during the warmer months.

1

Over that weekend, Bruce told me stories of the Clark family and the lives they lived - stories that he had heard from his parents who had spent summers on Ligonier Point since 1924. Initially, they vacationed in the old quarry worker's schoolhouse and, subsequently, they acquired the quarry master's house, Scragwood. The stories he related piqued my innate curiosity and fed directly into my lifelong love of history. For the next three years, we spent weekends and vacations salvaging and hastily storing everything that we could from an old icehouse as it slowly sank into the earth below and would soon be nothing but a fragile shell. All manner of memorabilia from stacks of correspondence to photographs, books to discarded pieces of furniture, and even an unused coffin, lay jumbled together in heaps on the damp earthen floor.

Finally, in 2001 we left city and professional lives behind and took up permanent residency on Ligonier Point. At last, I was able to step aside as an educator and put my college degree in American Cultural History to use. Did I have any concept of what lay ahead of me? Definitely not! Did I know that every building and outbuilding on our property was filled with historical gems that were just waiting to be discovered? Not at all! If I had known I might not have had the courage to move forward and tackle what awaited me.

One by one, we opened shutters and unlocked doors, exposing the contents of each structure to light and air, and awakening them from their slumbers. Remnants of the past were hidden in nooks and crannies, beneath floors, inside walls, in attics and cellars, tucked away in old steamer trunks, and even behind books of a more contemporary nature. Dresser drawers and chests overflowed with beautiful quilts, linens and clothing that had been made by hand so many years ago, and boxes of china and crystal that had been stored away for decades revealed their beautiful contents that were lovingly collected over several generations. At last, objects that had lain hidden from the outside world for almost a century were coming to life again.

While I stood in awe, amazement, and feeling quite overwhelmed by it all, historian and author, Morris Glenn, stepped into my life and provided the guidance and oversight that I so desperately needed. With each passing day as we worked together the pile of articles and artifacts, dating from 1759 to 1920, grew at a truly alarming rate, provoking Morris to continually remark, "This is the gift that won't stop giving." To date, we have amassed over 51,000 letters, business records, diaries, architectural and engineering drawings, letters, and a wide variety of other paper items: almost 1,000 books, pamphlets, magazines and periodicals; over 6,000 photographs; and 2,100 textiles. Each has been handled with respect and loving care, categorized, conserved, archived, and shared with others through tours, presentations and written materials that Morris and I have prepared.

As we worked through the abundance before us, questions kept bubbling up to the surface. We found answers to some, but certainly not all. Who were these Clarks who lived and worked amid the rocks, on the land, on the lake, and in those old buildings? What sorts of endeavors did they engage in? What were their daily lives like? Were they educated? Were they religious? Did they participate in local affairs? How were they viewed within their community? Did they ever travel beyond the shores of Lake Champlain? Were they participants in the making of regional and national history? What did they contribute that was truly lasting and meaningful? The list of questions went on and on. We don't pretend to have all of the answers yet - and maybe we never will – but we do have an ever-increasing understanding of the Clarks and the "world" in which they lived.

Our belief that we had true historical treasures before us was confirmed by those far more knowledgeable than we. Bruce and I knew that we had to make certain that the Clark Collection and their structures would survive for the generations to come, and that they would be loved, cared for and used by many. In 2013, Scragwood, the quarry master's home, received a historic preservation award from Adirondack Architectural Heritage (AARCH), the former

Clark property was designated a National Historic District by the United States Department of the Interior, and the newly-restored walled garden at Scragwood was listed in the Smithsonian Archives of American Gardens. In that same year, we established a not-for-profit historical research foundation chartered as an Education Corporation under the New York State Board of Regents. Our mission was to facilitate the interpretation of the agricultural, industrial, maritime, economic, social, and cultural history of Willsboro and its surrounding areas' inhabitants, to enhance a deeper understanding and appreciation of that history, and to promote public access and scholarly research. The Foundation Board worked tirelessly to find a permanent home for the Clark Collection that would meet these criteria. Now, in 2018, it is on its way to the New York State Library where it will be properly maintained and, more importantly, it will be digitized so that the rich history of the Clarks of Willsboro Point can be shared with all.

With excitement and, yes, even some trepidation, after almost eighteen years of discovery, caretaking and research, a voice within me grew louder and more insistent. It was time for me tell the story - a story that commences wrapped in the misty folds of mystery and unknowns, and then over time gathers momentum and clarity as it moves forward. Over those years, the story has evolved and grown within me, as each day I have stepped back in time, and almost become a nineteenth century Clark. Each document, each picture, and each drawing and record has become a part of me.

Now I have the privilege of telling their story as best I can. Early records of Willsboro, New York, and of the Clark family in particular, are scant in places throughout the period of 1800 to about 1850. There are some voids that may remain so forever, as well as some pieces that will always be a bit ragged around the edges like a newly quarried bit of stone. Thus, of necessity my descriptions draw upon primary source materials wherever possible, but also include elements of historical conjecture that are based upon the research opportunities available to me. Beyond that, I have drawn upon my imagination, and filled in personal observations and thoughts as well as actions and details.

By 1850, the amount of raw material at my fingertips expands exponentially and the wealth of materials before me can tell the story on their own. We will have travelled through the lives of George and Lydia in Book I of the series, and moved on into the young life of their son Orrin. In Book II, Orrin is a grown man and father who has built a stately home for himself and his family and has continued to practice farming just as his "adopted father" trained him to do. In Book III, the story increasingly revolves around his eldest sons, Solomon the bluestone quarry master and Lewis a marine architect and shipbuilder. Their wives and children feature as do some of the other, less well-known members of the family. As I continue telling the story, there may even be a Book IV that focuses upon the waning years of the Clarks on Willsboro Point. Who knows!

I invite you to come with me on my journey, to rejoice with the Clarks in the happy times, to suffer along with those whose lives were too often grim and short, to be inspired by the will and fortitude of these rugged people, to understand what kept them alive and functioning through thick and thin, to feel what they felt, and to experience what they experienced, as we follow them through their daily lives. Whether you are a historian, researcher, or someone who is just plain interested in history and the people who created it, I hope that you will join me as my story unfolds.

Darcey Hale
Willsboro, New York
July 4, 2018

THE SCENE IS SET

In 1758, the King of Great Britain authorized colonial governors to issue land grants, particularly to those who had served in the French and Indian War.[1] William Gilliland, an Irish merchant who was living in New York City, was the recipient of such a grant and had agents scouting for land that he could purchase on the western shore of Lake Champlain. By 1765, his purchases included significant landholdings that had been surveyed. At that point, he determined to leave New York City to establish his claims on a permanent basis. On May 10, 1765, he left to formalize his claims, taking with him a preacher, two millwrights, a carpenter, a clerk, a weaver and others. At Albany, they embarked in four bateaux that were laden with people and stores.[2] They arrived at their destination on the Boquet River on June 8, 1765 and immediately set about clearing forest, cutting wood, building a small wing dam, and squaring timber for a mill. Soon they began laying out building lots for those settlers who were following them. By November 4, Gilliland was on his way back to New York City, leaving the other settlers to continue their work until he got back the following spring. On June 22, 1766 he, his wife, daughter, various other relatives and twenty-two wagons of stores and furniture arrived back in Milltown (his name for the settlement). Tragically, another daughter, Elizabeth, had drowned off Stillwater on the trip. The colony continued to grow and, by March of 1775, was grappling with the "need for regulations concerning fences, bridges, roads and hogs."[3]

By 1777, with the conflict between the British and Americans at its height Gilliland had ruffled many feathers for a variety of reasons. Ultimately, he ran afoul of Benedict Arnold who accused him of fraud and disloyalty, claiming that Gilliland was really a Loyalist and not a true patriot. Later it was proven that this was not the case, but the animosities remained. At this same time, Ethan Allen and Benedict Arnold were engaged in rivalries of their own and Gilliland was caught in the midst of all this.[4] During that year, while Arnold was patrolling the lake prior to Burgoyne's defeat by Carleton he let his men "land [at Milltown] and ravage crops without restraint."[5] It appears that they laid waste to the land and all but about twenty settlers fled for their lives. As if this were not enough, as Burgoyne and his troops were retreating to Canada they were attacked by Captain Ebenezer Allen [brother of Ethan] as they were ravaging what remained of Gilliland's settlement. Captain Allen "captured forty-nine British soldiers, one hundred horses, twelve yokes of oxen, three boats and one black slave belonging to Gilliland. Court records in Bennington, Vermont showed that some of the forty-nine British soldiers were actually residents of Gilliland's settlement who were alleged to be Loyalists. As a punitive measure, Allen burned the remaining buildings in Gilliland's settlement.[6] Thus, Gilliland and his settlement became the victims of a variety of political conflicts and misunderstandings. Ultimately, Gilliland himself was arrested on charges of treason levied against him by Arnold and he was sent to prison in Albany in January of 1778. He filed a complaint stating that he had been mistreated unjustly to no avail. For the next three years, nothing was heard from or about his whereabouts or whether he had been released from prison at some point during this time period.[7]

With the close of the War, the Champlain Valley was opening up to settlers at a rapid rate and Gilliland, who had been freed from prison, was getting many applications for land grants from his vast holdings. He would have had the opportunity to garner significant financial rewards except for the fact that he had never secured patents for his lands. This left them wide open to others. Thereafter, he tried various schemes in which to recover financially but was never successful.[8] When he returned to the site of his former colony in 1783, he found a virtual wasteland. By 1786, his efforts to retain some control had become totally futile, and ultimately, he wound up in prison in New York City because of his efforts to regain his slaves and other misdeeds. A basically destitute, broken and depressed man he was released from prison once again in 1792. He went to live with his son-in-law Daniel Ross who was married to his daughter Jane. Sadly, his life ended tragically when he lost his way in a snowstorm in 1796 and died on Split Rock Mountain.[9]

As the War of Independence drew to a close, former settlers began to return to their homes to face many years of labor to reclaim their land and rebuild Gilliland's former village. A total of sixteen families had returned to the area and purchased land from Gilliland.[10] A group of about twenty-six early settlers gathered together in the home of Melchor Hoffnagel's house in April 1788 to officially establish the Town of Willsborough in Clinton County, which comprised over 900 square miles at that time. They included Abraham Aiken, John and Melchor Hoffnagel, John Morhous, Stephen Taylor, Jonathan Lynde, Daniel Sheldon, Stephen Cuyler, Joseph and Daniel Sheldon, Samuel Brown, Levi Cooley, and others. Melchor was elected the town's first Supervisor, Daniel Sheldon was its Clerk and Daniel Ross was sheriff. Since there was no official town building, town meetings were held in the homes of various citizens for the purpose of establishing regulations and electing town officials. [11]

By 1790, Platt Rogers, an entrepreneur who controlled many transactions in northern New York had built a road that connected the ferry landing to the south and the town of Willsborough. In the town, he constructed a two-span wood bridge, with an island in between, over the Boquet river and then another road that went over the mountain, through Chesterfield and then on north to Peru.[12] This was critical to the future growth and prosperity of the new town. Roads were being built in rapid succession thereafter, and served as vital links between landowners, small settlements and beyond the confines of the town. By this time, John Hoffnagle had opened a store several miles north of the ferry landing and

John Morhous had built the first store within the village itself.[13] There were an abundance of inns and taverns throughout the settlement and six of these settlers, including Jonathan Lynde and Stephen Taylor, had been granted licenses.[14] Now that roads connected the various towns, and goods could even be brought across the lake, both of these stores had a means of obtaining a host of items that community members needed and were not able to produce for themselves. This was especially important since their only other way to procure goods was from peddlers, who made occasional visits as they followed their routes throughout the region.

Also, by the mid-1790s a road out to Willsborough Point had been built and settlers began to move out there to take advantage of supposed "free" land. These early settlers were mere squatters, although they were loath to admit this and took the land as their own. They had no real right to property since it was still part of the original Montresor Patent. Among them were the Adsits (Jacob, Samuel and Kenyon), Asa Fisher, William Stroud, Daniel Bacon, Samuel Barney, and Truman Nash. These early families lived in rough log cabins which they built using the abundance of virgin timber that lay before them. While logging to build dwellings and outbuildings, they were also opening up land for pastures and crops for their livestock. Since they were removed some five miles from the town itself they formed an informal community of their own which became known as "The Point".[15]

In 1798, Willsborough was still part of Clinton County and portions of its 900 square miles began to be split off into separate parcels. The first split resulted in the formation of Keene and Chesterfield. Just a year later, in 1799, Essex County was formed as a separate entity.[16] In that same year, Daniel Ross was appointed the first Judge of the Essex County Court of Common Pleas. He was also appointed as the county's first sheriff, having served in this capacity as well as being a member of the county council prior to the formation of Essex County. He convened his court in the log blockhouse near McNeil's sail ferry dock that was also used to hold prisoners. The blockhouse had been built soon after the end of the Revolution as a means of protecting the local inhabitants from Indian uprisings.[17] There had been no uprisings, so the conversion of its usage had been appropriate.

Despite the fact that the original boundaries of the town had shrunk, the population continued to grow as more and more settlers came to the area. The 1800 census indicated that there were fifty-three householders and 500 inhabitants in Willsborough.[18] Daniel Ross had been granted considerable land along the Boquet by his father-in-law William Gilliland.[19] He had taken full advantage of the force of the water going over the rapids at Willsborough and over the new wing dam that he had built to provide power for his proposed Anchor Shop which will be featured later.

As an interesting side note, there appears to have been slaveholders in the area at that time. According to Levy Higby, a prominent citizen, some of the wealthier citizens in the area were slaveholders. He said that he had heard that there were about sixty slaves in Clinton County and he did not know how many there might be in Essex County.[20] He did know for a fact that in 1801 Judge Daniel Ross had certified that "On the first day of August in the year 1801 Jack a male negro child was born and is the son of a negro wench who is my property."[21]

By the fall of 1801, when George Clark and his family, who are the focus of this book, arrived in Willsborough, the town government had established a number of official positions to ensure that its affairs were properly regulated. Male citizens now served in capacities such as supervisor, clerk, assessor, constable, collector, and highway supervisor. In addition, there were poor masters who loaned money with interest to those in need, pound keepers who handled miscreant livestock, damage appraisers who handled disputes over loss or damage done by one property owner to another, and fence viewers who handled property line disputes. Many of these appointees had community members who worked under them.[22] In that same year, as the numbers of roads continued to proliferate, highway districts were established. Orders were given to all male citizens that "You are hereby commanded to come every man to work the whole number of days next to his name."[23]

LIVES INTERTWINED

Our story begins in Canaan, Litchfield County, Connecticut; a remote and spread out farming community that sits on the southwestern edge of the Berkshire Mountains and straddles the Massachusetts-Connecticut border. By the mid-eighteenth century, the village center had a sawmill, grist mill, fulling mill,[24] where wool was shrunk in order to make its weave tighter and more weatherproof, and an ironworks,[25] all of which took advantage of the natural falls on the Housatonic River which the Indians called "Place Beyond the Mountains."[26] George Clark, the future patriarch of the Clark family, was born there on January 7, 1777.[27] He came from a long line of farmers who had tilled the land in this part of Connecticut for generations.

George's father, like many of the men and older boys in Canaan, set out to fight for the independence of their country. The women of Canaan banded together as they struggled to keep their families together without a man. When at last, the Canaan men and boys who had survived the conflict returned to their homes there was much rejoicing. Bit by bit, bound by their deep sense of community, their frugal ways, and their profound belief in the will of God, the families began piecing together the threads of their lives as they undertook the painful process of rebuilding and restoring order to their fragmented world.

Soon, Canaan was a thriving small town once again with many of its former businesses and farms up and running as they had before. Being of farm stock, young George had taken his place working the land, along with his father and siblings, and upon occasion, when the demands of the farm were not great, he was able to attend the local school that was taught by an itinerant preacher. Like most boys in Canaan, his education was rudimentary, but would suffice in the arena in which he lived and worked. As a teenager, his father also allowed him to work in the nearby iron works when he could spare him. This provided a bit of much-needed outside income for the family. George developed some strong skills working with iron, but working the land remained his long-term goal.

Like most young people, George looked forward to the occasions upon which he and his friends from Canaan, and the surrounding communities, could get together to socialize. The centerpiece for these was often the town's Congregational meetinghouse, and there George became acquainted with Lydia Jakeways, daughter of Phineas and Hannah Jakeways. Lydia's parents had moved from Canaan to Stillwater, New York when she was just four years old. During her occasional visits back to Canaan she discovered how wonderful it was to be where she had so many relatives. She became particularly attached to her aunt and uncle who persuaded her parents to let twelve-year-old Lydia come to live with them for a bit. She loved being embraced by so many family members and soon began to make friends with many of the local girls. This was rapidly becoming home for her.

When Lydia was old enough to be "hired out" to other family members, so that she could learn the housekeeping skills that were essential to her future as a good wife and mother, she moved from one family to another. Fortunately, her experiences with all of these families were happy ones. A highlight of her week was going to church on Sundays and, even more so, attending the church socials. The years went on in this vein for Lydia until she met a young farmer and part-time bloomer named George Clark. As she and George became better acquainted, their friendship developed into love, and on April 23, 1794, George took Lydia's hand in marriage.[28] He was but seventeen and his bride was twenty-two.

Following their marriage, the young couple set up housekeeping with George's parents in Canaan. George continued to work on his father's farm where he spent his days tilling the soil, harvesting the fruits of his labors, tending the livestock, making and maintaining the tools he needed, and doing the multitude of chores that consumed a farmer's days from dawn to dusk. On occasion, he returned to the iron works when they were in great need of help.

Lydia shared the household burdens with her mother-in-law as she went about addressing the seemingly endless daily tasks of childcare, cooking, cleaning, washing, ironing, sewing, helping with lighter farm chores, and even butchering. Before dawn she arose to light the woodstove and assist in preparing a hearty morning meal for the menfolk. From then on it seemed that she barely had time to complete her morning's household work before the hungry men were marching in the door to take a break and indulge in the bounteous noon repast that had been prepared for them. Following this main meal men and women alike returned to their round of chores before the family came together once again to enjoy a lighter evening repast before retiring for the night.

Within less than a year of their marriage, Lydia bore her first child on February 28, 1795. She was grateful for all that she had learned about taking care of a baby during the years before Polly's arrival, and glad that she was still in the family home where the older women gave her guidance and support. The years rolled by and three years later Orrin was born on January 2, 1798.[29] Life continued much has it had for them. George remained a helpful and productive member of his family and steadily put funds away with an eye to purchasing land of his own one day.

By June 19, 1799, he, at age twenty-two, had amassed enough capital to acquire a place of his own. For $8.94, he was able to purchase from Zacheus Wileas a small plot of land outside of New Marlborough, Massachusetts, a tiny hamlet in Berkshire County that lies just across the Connecticut border from Canaan. The land transaction was typical of its time with the property description reading "One certain part of the lot North of the Third Division situated in New Marlborough beginning at a stake and stone on the east side of the highway running east eight rods to a stake and stones then southerly ten rod ¾ of a rod to a stake and stones then westerly to a stake and stones on the highway then northerly on the highway ten rods ¾ to the first mentioned bounds, containing one half acre...this to be an absolute estate of inheritance in fee simple forever." As was common at that time, the land transaction was dated "In the twenty-third year of the Independence of the United States" rather than the actual year.[30] On the deed, George was listed as a bloomer which indicates that he had continued to work at the iron works in Canaan, in addition to working on his father's farm.

The young family had barely settled into their small, frame house and started getting accustomed to farming and housekeeping on their own before their second son, George, came into this world on September 11, 1799. Less than two years later, Sally was born on May 14, 1801.[31] Enveloped in their daily lives, the young couple lived from day to day with no realization that their time in New Marlborough would be very short-lived, and that fate and a tale of intertwining happenstances would soon intervene and change their lives radically.

Here we must leave the story of George and his family briefly and turn our attention to Levi Higby who will play a pivotal role in the lives of the young Clarks in the near future. Like George, Levi had grown up in Canaan and, as a young man, had worked on his family's farm. The two were almost the same age and attended the same small schoolhouse when family and farm chores did not intervene. Levi and George spent many happy hours together playing and fishing along the banks of the Housatonic, a river that flowed through Canaan and supplied vital waterpower for the various local industries. In addition, their parents were close friends, and often came together for community gatherings, so the boys had a quasi-familial relationship.

In 1794, Levi, like George, married a woman he had come to know at a church social. He took the hand of Chloe Cobb, a resident of Attleboro, Massachusetts whom he met when she came to Canaan to help take care of her cousin's children. Levi and Chloe settled into early-married life in Canaan, and in 1796 they brought a son, Alanson, into the world, and then, just a year later Levi Jr. was born on September 17, 1797. Throughout those very early years of marriage Levi and George and their wives remained close friends. However, soon after the birth of their second son Chloe and Levi left Canaan and headed west in search of cheaper and more readily available farmland. The young couple took up residence in Fort Ann, New York where Levi , like George Clark, was able to use the iron working skills that he had acquired from occasional work in the bloomery and as a farmer in Canaan.[32] During their time in Fort Ann, the Higbys became close friends of George Throop, who will also play a pivotal role in the future, and his wife.[33] Little did the Higby or the Throop families know that the friendship they formed in Fort Ann would keep them close to one another for the rest of their lives. Although unknown to either the Throops or the Higbys at the time, the lives of these two families would soon be changed radically by an outside force that meant little, if anything, to either of them.

The, as yet unknown, outside force was the series of bills that Congress passed between 1798 and 1800. These bills broadened the powers that had been granted in the 1794 Naval Act in order to protect American shipping interests from marauding pirates. In addition, on April 30, 1798 Congress passed an act that established an independent executive Department of the Navy whose responsibility was to further strengthen the earlier protection measures.[34] So, one asks, how would these things have had any impact upon the lives of two families residing in Fort Ann?

Here our story must take another twist and turn as it moves still further north to Willsborough, New York, a small village on the west bank of Lake Champlain. Daniel Ross, the son-in-law of William Gilliland, who first settled the community in

1765, was married to Gilliland's daughter Elizabeth. William had been granted land under the Montresor Patent in recognition of his service during the War of Independence. He, in turn, gave a portion this landholding to Daniel. When Daniel heard that the Navy would be greatly increasing its fleet in order to keep peace on the waters and marauding pirates at bay he joined forces with a land and business speculator from Schenectady, New York named Charles Kane. Together, they looked into ways in which to capitalize on this event and soon discovered that the Navy would be looking for a source of anchors for the fleet.

Daniel knew of an ideal place on his newly acquired land where he could locate a shop in which to make anchors. It was right where his father-in-law had established what he had called Milltown. There the waters of the Boquet River coursed swiftly as they made their way toward the open waters of Lake Champlain. As the river reached Willsborough, its waters plunged swiftly over rapids. This would be a perfect place to build a wing dam that would provide power for their enterprise.[35]

Daniel and Charles contacted the Navy and made such a convincing argument that they were awarded a contract to build all the anchors they could over a ten-year period. The finished anchors were to be shipped to Troy, New York from whence they would be forwarded to their ultimate destinations.[36]

In order to fulfill the terms of their contract with the Navy, Kane and Ross had to secure good management to oversee the construction of the Anchor Shop and, later, its operation. In some way, as yet unknown, Charles Kane had become acquainted with Levi Higby and George Throop in Fort Ann and knew that they were accomplished ironworkers. Upon Kane's recommendation, he and Daniel Ross offered Throop and Higby the opportunity to move north to Willsborough to become part of this new venture.[37] If things worked out favorably during the construction phase, they were promised full management of the operation once it was up and running.

With an opportunity like this before them neither George nor Levi hesitated in making the decision to uproot themselves and their families and move north to Willsborough despite the fact that it was in an area that was commonly referred to as the "Wilderness." With excitement, and some trepidation, the Throop and Higby families packed up their goods and left the comforts of Fort Ann behind them.

When they arrived, they were greeted by Daniel Ross who had already seen that each family had a domicile. Once their families were relatively settled in their new locale, Levi and George set about engaging workers who would construct the new Anchor Shop. Meanwhile Daniel Ross sought a reliable source of iron ore. He knew that there were small deposits of bog iron belonging to Platt Rogers to the north.[38] He figured that these would get the operation going until they could locate other, larger sources of ore.[39] As time went on, Daniel and Charles became increasingly impressed by the way in which Levi and George handled every aspect of building the Anchor Shop and, true to their word, they offered them permanent positions as managers of the operation.

While Levi and George were maintaining oversight of the construction, they also began the search for future employees. In order to get the operation up and running as quickly as possible, they realized that they would need to engage men who were skilled in working with iron, and Levi thought of his old friend George Clark who, like himself, had worked in the iron works in Canaan. Levi's parents assured him that George had grown into a reliable, honest and trustworthy man who was now married and a property owner across the Massachusetts border in New Marlborough. Levi sent word to his friend and offered him the opportunity for steady work over a long period of time, as well as the financial remuneration that the company would offer if he would come to Willsborough.

The offer that he received was exceedingly tempting to George. Although, financially, the decision to leave his newly acquired farm, and the area that he and his family had known throughout their lives seemed wise, it was heart wrenching nevertheless. George, Lydia and their children would be leaving lifelong friends and family behind and making a long, unpredictable journey northward to Willsborough. They would be settling in an unfamiliar place that George had been assured offered great promise for him and his family, but he could not help asking himself at what cost this might be. In the end, he determined that accepting the offer and making the move presented opportunities that he would not have if he remained where he had always lived. At this point our story brings Levi Higby and George Clark together once again.

One can only imagine that the prospect of a brighter future was all that mitigated the fear that George and Lydia felt in the months preceding their departure. The journey alone presented a daunting prospect with three small children - six-year-old Polly, three-year-old Orrin, and two-year-old George - as well as their infant daughter, Sally, who had just recently been born on May 14, 1801. George knew that he and his family must depart in August if there was to be any chance of completing the journey before colder weather began to set in, with winter close behind it. He set about arranging his affairs, successfully sold his property in New Marlborough, and left farming life behind – at least for the foreseeable future. George and Lydia headed down to Canaan as soon as they could after Sally's birth. They intended to make their final preparations for the journey living with George's family as they had done before their move to New Marlborough. They both wanted to spend a last bit of time with their relatives and friends in Canaan since they could not help wondering if they would ever see any of them again.

Lydia and George marveled at how quickly their young brood seemed to be able to adapt to changes in their lives. As long as they had friends and family around them, food to eat, and a place to sleep they were quite satisfied with their lives. The young couple couldn't help feeling a bit envious of this special gift that so many children seem to have. This, alone, gave them hope that the biggest move of any of their lives would go well.

As the day of departure loomed closer, George turned his attention to the many plans to be made, and details to be thought out. With no other real option, he knew that for the journey he must use the sturdy farm wagon that had served him well in New Marlborough to transport his family, as well as their provisions and possessions. His trusty yoke of oxen would pull the wagon, and he planned to ride alongside on horseback, occasionally moving ahead to scout out the terrain and figure out the best route or predict the best way to get around any obstacles that might lie beyond view.

Because they were only able to glean scant accurate information about the areas they would be passing through on their way to Willsborough, George knew that he had to be prepared for a wide variety of possible eventualities. He considered what they would need to take with them, and then tried to figure out the most expedient way in which to pack the wagon. He constructed a crude wood shell over which he laid a canvas cover to shield his family and possessions from rain and glaring sun as much as possible. Then, he built racks along its sides that would further help to support the canvas cover and would hold pots and pans for cooking, storage for provisions, and places for the boxes and crates to hold their belongings. He even built a portable coop to carry a rooster, as well as some hens that he hoped would be inclined to lay eggs despite being enclosed and jostled around during the journey.

They could not be certain of how long their journey would take, or how many opportunities they might have to renew their provisions, so Lydia put as many stores of foods as possible in the wagon. She, George's mother, and her aunt with whom she had lived previously, had worked together to prepare things from their gardens, and had dried and pickled some of the produce. They used straw to protect and preserve their foodstuffs for as long as possible, they packed a few fresh vegetables and berries and stowed them in the coolest spot they could find amongst the straw, and then they laid in some dried and pickled vegetables. George and his father had slaughtered several pigs, and salted or smoked the meat for the journey, along with some fish that they had caught down on the river and had salted down heavily. These were also carefully packed in boxes of straw. Lydia made sure to include some herbs, as well as a few spices, that would improve the flavor of their food and disguise the rancid taste of items that were a bit over the hill, as well as serving medicinal purposes when needed.

They had filled sacks with the beans, split peas and corn that Lydia's aunt had dried from the previous year's crop, as well as boxes with apples and pears from their old orchard back in New Marlborough that they had cut and dried in the previous autumn evenings. They stowed sacks of cornmeal, oatmeal and bran, and added jars of molasses and vinegar, wherever they could find space. Of course, Lydia made sure that she had a good stock of flour, lard, sugar, and the saleratus that was necessary to make her bread rise. She put in tea and coffee, and also laid in a supply of freshly preserved jams, as well as honey from her aunt's apiary. These would be perfect with the breads and biscuits that she planned to bake over an open fire on the journey.[40]

With the foodstuffs taken care of, George finished packing the wagon. First, he laid a bed of straw on the floorboards to soften the jolting and jarring that was inevitable, and then he covered the straw with old sheets. Next came the feather bed that he and Lydia treasured, and a pile of blankets and quilts for padding, and for warmth when needed. He filled the remaining racks and shelves to the brim with the cooking vessels, crockery, utensils and other household items that Lydia had laid out for him. The children clamored for a few of their most precious playthings to be put on board, and so these were added to the growing pile. With everything safely stowed away, there was just a wee bit of room left for a very few treasured items which neither he nor Lydia could bear to leave behind. Finally, George carefully loaded the precious family Bible on board. This would remind them of home when they were far away.

George was well aware that his travels would be very dependent upon the road conditions. He had been warned by itinerants and peddlers who came to Canaan that the roads to the north and west were sometimes mere tracks. He was told that there were few inns along the way, except for those in larger towns, so it was important for them to be prepared to spend their nights along the roadsides. There, he would need to look out for thieves who were not afraid to steal anything they could find. Wolves also presented a danger to both animals and people. This information made George very certain that he needed to have a good, reliable rifle with him at all times.

From his experience as a farmer taking a fully loaded wagon to a nearby town, he had learned that he and his team of oxen could travel about three miles in an hour. Based upon this information, he figured that they should be able to go about twelve to fifteen miles in a day and hoped that, if they had to push harder, they might be able to cover twenty miles. Of course, all of this was based upon the premise that the road conditions would be adequate. Because he was traveling in the late summer months, he had promise of better weather, but he knew that this would not always be the case. Endless days without rain would turn the roads into dustbowls that covered people and animals, as well as the wagon and its contents, with itchy, grimy grains of dirt that had a habit of getting into every nook and cranny.

With the slightest rain, the roads that were hard-packed would quickly turn into quagmires of mud into which his team could find themselves up to their bellies, and the wagon wheels could become totally encased right up to their axles, or even above. Every traveler's fear was a road that had become a type of primeval swamp that simply sucked anything that passed over it into the ooze that lay beneath. This would cause significant damage to their wagon, scatter its contents far and wide, injure his team of oxen and his horse, and cause great delays in travel. On the other hand, endless days without rain would turn the roads into dustbowls that covered people and animals, as well as a wagon and its contents, with itchy, grimy grains of dirt that had a habit of getting into every nook and cranny.[41] They simply had to pray for more good days than bad.

George worried about his family on this journey. He knew

that this would make for a long, tough day with Lydia and the children confined in the wagon and realized that he needed to factor in a few stops along the way so that the children could get out to run a bit, and Lydia and baby Sally could get some relief from the constant jolting of the wagon as it ran over tree stumps and ruts, and all manner of impediments that the roads presented. He had been careful not to share all that he was learning with Lydia because he was certain that she would be filled with terrible anxiety for herself and the children. She would find out all too soon. For now, she had enough on her mind just coping with the fact that she was leaving behind everything that she had ever known. George could only pray that the trip would go well for them all.

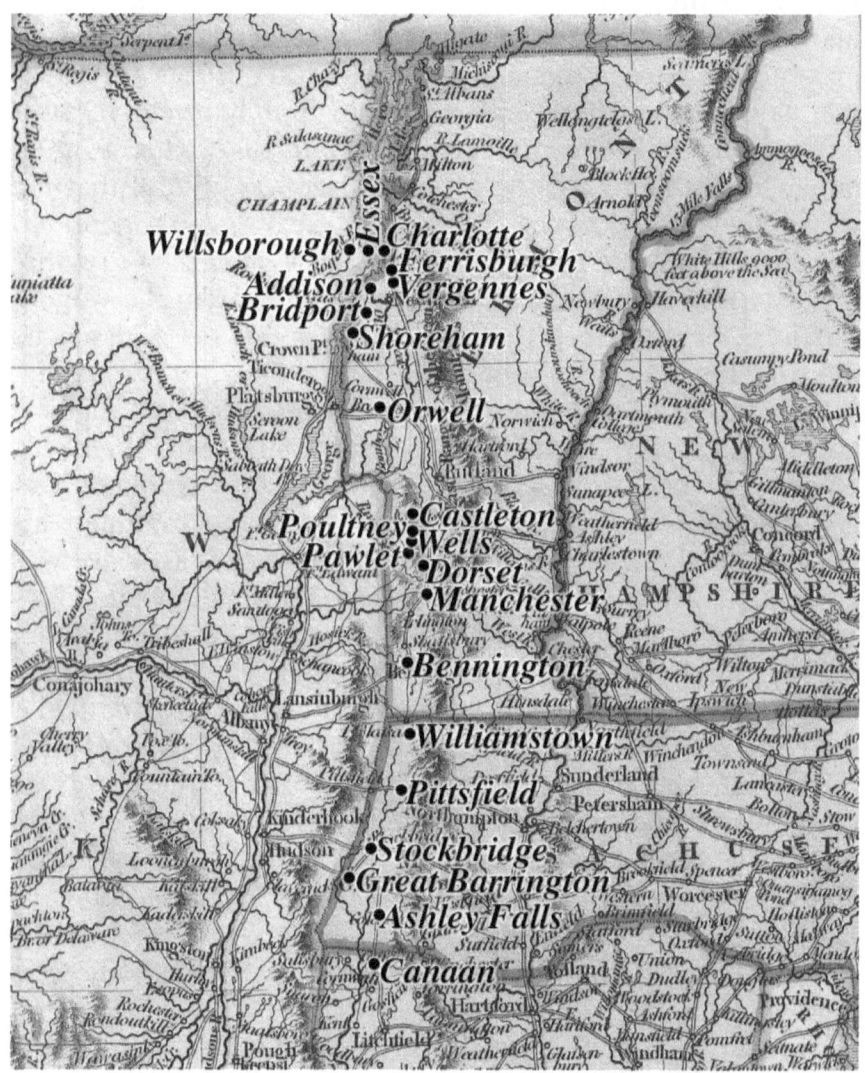

The Clarks' Trek North. 1820 Map of Northeastern USA.

Following the weeks of preparation, the day of their departure arrived. The weather was fair, which they took to be a good omen for the journey. In the predawn hour, when George and his family arose, the air was still cool with just a hint that the warmth of the season would soon be upon them. With all in readiness, six-year-old Polly jumped up onto the wagon excitedly chattering about the adventure that lay ahead. Three-year-old Orrin and his year-younger brother George were not so sure about all of this as their father lifted them onto the wagon. They were fretful that the world they had known in their short lives was going to disappear. However, they felt a bit better when they saw that their favorite toys had truly been stashed away in the wagon. Finally, George helped Lydia on board giving her a kiss as he did so. Clutching three-month-old infant, Sally, to her bosom, she tried to settle into the somewhat comfortable nest that she had created for them among the quilts and blankets. Goodbyes were said, tears were shed, and they were ready at last. George yoked up his steadfast oxen and mounted his horse. A final few words of farewell were said, a last wave was given to family and friends, and they were on their way.

By talking to others who had recently travelled further afield than he had, George had been able to work out a tentative route north. He had been told that the particular roads he planned to travel over were a bit better maintained than most, and there was enough vehicular traffic to ensure some degree of safety from marauders. However, there would still be the need to be constantly vigilant for attacks by wild animals that could hurt them, as well as their own animals. He prayed that, as much as possible, the weather would be fair and the roads would remain passable throughout their journey.

He had been advised to head north from Canaan, passing through Ashley Falls in Massachusetts, and on into Great Barrington. From there he would proceed further north through Stockbridge and, finally, to Pittsfield where he would need to make a decision about the next leg of his journey.

Based upon what information he had been able to glean, George figured that they would need to cover about forty miles or so to get to Pittsfield. This would involve two very long, hard days. After getting a bit later start than anticipated on this, the first day of their journey, George decided to go only as far as the other side of Ashley Falls, on the Housatonic River, which lay just twelve miles away. Fortunately, at this time of year the sun did not go below the horizon until quite late and the roads, although rutted, were in fairly good condition which made their travels easier. He decided that it would be judicious to take three days to get to Pittsfield rather than the two that he had planned originally.

In the late afternoon, they passed through Ashley Falls, and just on the other side of the village they found a quiet place, close to the road on the banks of the river, where they could rest for the night. Everyone was tired, and the children were a bit cranky after being cooped up in the wagon for the first time. Even this short distance was far longer than any time that they had ever had to spend like this.

George quickly helped everyone down from the wagon, and even two-year-old George was permitted to get down so long as he stayed close to his father. Lydia remained in the wagon just long enough to nurse Sally and snuggle her down comfortably so that she would be free to attend to the evening repast. Under Polly's watchful eye, Orrin was allowed to go down to the banks of the river and dip his little toes into the flowing water.

George's first task was to build a fire upon which Lydia could cook their meal. He gathered small branches and twigs and put them in a circle that he built in a small clearing a short distance away from the wagon and other trees. With this done, he put other small bits of twigs in the tinderbox that he carried with him and struck a piece of flint to his steel until he had enough spark to ignite the fire he had laid. He then turned to tend to his other chores. Lydia made sure that baby Sally was asleep and then went about preparing the evening repast. If they were at home, they would have had their main meal of the day at midday. However, this was not practical when one was traveling. During their journey it would be necessary to have only a noon repast consisting of dried fruits, nuts, bread, jam and an occasional bit of fresh wild fruit, if they were able to find any. This would enable them to keep traveling throughout the day without interruption, except to water and rest the animals, let everyone out of the wagon briefly to stretch their legs, and make any necessary adjustments to the wagon and its load.

While Lydia was busy with her preparations, George went about seeing that his animals were secure. He tied them to some nearby trees where they could graze peacefully and hung a lantern from a nearby branch that he would ignite later. This would provide light throughout the night so that he could see any animal or person that might approach. With no rain in sight, they were able to partake of their evening meal outdoors instead of being cramped in the wagon or under the small bit of canvas George had brought for a makeshift tent. He found a couple of old logs on which they could sit while Lydia finished the final preparations of their meal. She had put together a hearty stew of slabs of salt pork, some carrots and onions from the garden back home, and a big chunk of bread that she had stowed in the wagon. Soon, this was steaming over the open fire and a delicious aroma wafted through the air. As they ate, they huddled as close to the fire as possible to ward off the mosquitos that inevitably assembled around them at dusk.

After the evening's meal was complete, Lydia took the cooking and eating vessels and utensils down to the river's edge where she cleaned them off in preparation for the next evening's meal. Finally, everything was set for the night and George wearily climbed into the wagon to settle down next to Lydia and the baby. Each of the children had found his or her special place to curl up and spend this night and the nights ahead. George got as much sleep as he could, but he could not help worrying about his animals that were outside, as well as the next day's travel.

At dawn, they arose to find that all was well. After eating some of Lydia's delicious bread with jam and a bit of butter, they set off on the day's journey. From Ashley Falls they picked up the Greenwood Road that they had been told had just been built two years before and, therefore, was in excellent condition. It went along the east side of the Housatonic to Great Barrington, through Pittsfield and headed northeast toward Albany, New York.[42] Because of the better road, and another sunny day, George hoped to be able to travel through Great Barrington and on into Stockbridge in one day - a distance of about twenty miles. On the road north, they picked their way through valleys that cut through the mountainous Berkshires.

Occasionally, George would stop the wagon to water the animals in the river or stream and let them rest a bit. This gave Polly, Orrin, and little George a chance to climb down for a bit of play before resuming the journey. From time to time, when Sally was asleep, Lydia would also alight in order to stretch her legs or to walk alongside the wagon for a bit. Despite the seeming paucity of homesteads in the area, periodically they would see signs, like a wisp of smoke in the air, that indicated that settlers were beginning to take full advantage of the natural resources that even this rugged terrain offered them. Upon occasion, a sawmill, or grist mill or even a small iron forge would appear. Toward dusk, George and the family reached Stockbridge where they could rest for a bit after the long journey through some steep and often fairly rough terrain. They followed the routine of the previous evening just as they would for many nights to come.

The next day, at the first light of dawn, the animals became restless, as they always did, and even the rooster began to crow loudly to announce the arrival of another morning. After Lydia dressed the children, she let them have an opportunity to run freely as long as they remained within her sight. While baby Sally slept, Lydia stole these precious moments to tidy up the wagon as best she could. She was grateful that she and George had taken great pains to carefully organize this tiny space before they started their journey. Meanwhile, George watered and fed his oxen and horse, as well as the hens that were squawking in their coops and still refusing to lay a single egg. With the chores done, the family came together for their usual brief morning repast. Soon the wagon was loaded, the oxen were yoked, the horse was saddled, and they were off once again. Fortunately, they were blessed with yet another fine day; this time with a light breeze that kept the flying insects away. It seemed like they covered the miles to the outskirts of Stockbridge more rapidly than the trip the day before.

On day three, as they were becoming more accustomed to the routine of travel, the hours and days began to slip away more quickly. The fifteen miles between Stockbridge and Pittsfield were covered without incident, and soon they found themselves in a thriving community with yet another abundance of sawmills, iron forges, and grist mills along the banks of the Housatonic. Here, the Greenwood Road, on which they had been traveling since they left Ashley Falls, turned west toward Albany. It had begun to drizzle soon after they got to Pittsfield and George decided that it would be best for them to seek one of the many taverns and inns in this town of 2,000 residents, where they could wait out the rainstorm. He had been told that innkeepers were always happy to let a traveler, with wagon and its occupants, spend a night in their enclosed yard. This was all for a fee, of course. They enjoyed a break in their routine of the past several days and had a bit to eat in a nearby tavern before retiring to their wagon for the night's repose. George was especially grateful that for this one night he did not need to be on guard constantly in order to ensure the security of his family and his livestock.

Because a heavy rain continued throughout the night, and into the day, Lydia and George decided to spend an additional day in Pittsfield with hopes that the weather would clear before they proceeded on their journey. After Canaan, this seemed like a huge metropolis to them. Lydia had some things from the farm that she could trade in order to get the few provisions they needed. The children loved running through the streets and peeking into the windows of shops that were filled with delectable looking candies, cakes, and other confections that made their mouths fairly water. They came upon a shop with all sorts of toys on display and, after many entreaties, George finally gave in and bought them each a small toy to help them while away the hours of the long journey that still lay ahead of them. Tired, but happy, with bellies filled with the food that they had procured in the shops, the family curled up in the wagon for a good night's sleep.

With Lydia and the children safely tucked in for the night, George went in to talk to the innkeeper about the best route for him to follow on the next leg of his journey. The innkeeper was constantly in contact with travelers and, therefore, was a good repository of information about the various roadways that went out from Pittsfield in all directions. He was touting the virtues of the newly-constructed Rensselaer Turnpike that linked Pittsfield and Albany. He assured George that this route would offer him and his family travel over a better and safer road than if he continued on his planned route north. However, as George thought about it, he realized that going to Albany would take him west of where he wanted to go rather than north. More importantly, he knew that this turnpike, like the others that were being built at a rapid rate throughout New England, was constructed by private investors who were looking for a considerable return on their investment. Because the Rensselaer Turnpike was a vital link between two thriving cities, it was especially costly.[43]   After taking into consideration all of the information that he had received, George decided to continue as planned, heading north through Williamstown and on into Bennington.

The day was fair so George and Lydia prepared to resume their journey as quickly as possible. He was hopeful that in one day they would be able to travel the twenty miles to Williamstown. Because of the recent rainfall, the going was a bit muddy for the first five miles or so, but it was not so bad that the wagon wheels sank down deeply. It did mean that its occupants were jolted around a bit more than usual, but they were getting used to that just as they were quickly getting in tune with the routines of travel. Even the team of oxen and George's horse were settling into the rhythm of the day, and after the initial few miles, the road proved to be well traveled and in good condition. Just south of Williamstown, George stopped to find a place that would be a satisfactory resting spot for the night. He found a nice grove of trees alongside a quietly flowing brook and thought that this would be an ideal spot since it provided some shelter for them, as well as a drinking opportunity for his livestock. The evening's routine was much like the days before, and George hoped that the days ahead would go as well.

Awakened as usual by their faithful cock, the Clarks arose early and went through their morning ritual before setting out for Bennington in Vermont, which was only twelve miles ahead. This was the last state that they would pass through before reaching their ultimate destination, New York. Much to their relief, they had been told that this part of their journey would be relatively smooth since Bennington was a major crossroads for routes going in all directions. They planned to spend the following day acquiring the essential provisions they would need for the next leg of their journey.

When they reached Bennington, a friendly town citizen pointed them toward Dewey's Tavern, a welcoming looking old clapboard structure that took in a few guests and had plenty of room for livestock as well as wagons and their occupants in the yard outside. The tavern keeper told them to make themselves comfortable while he prepared a bit of supper for them and, needless to say, Lydia delighted at the thought of not having to prepare a meal along the roadside.

In the morning, as they wandered through the town they saw many tributes to those who had fought at the Battle of Bennington, about twelve miles out of town. They were told that the outcome of the battle fought on August 16, 1777, was a decisive Revolutionary War victory for the rebels. The Townspeople were very proud of their heritage and were eager to share their town's stories of bravery and battle. George and Lydia quickly realized that this was a larger, more bustling and prosperous town than any that they had encountered before. Everywhere they looked there were wagons being heaped high with farm produce in preparation for heading to markets in Albany, Boston, and elsewhere. The place was teeming with carriages and people rushing hither and yon. There were street vendors hawking their wares and entertainers displaying their talents on almost every street corner. Never had any of them seen so much activity in one place and they were truly awestruck.

While in Bennington, George had received advice regarding the best route for them to follow as they continued on their journey northward, so the next day they headed for Manchester. As the days passed by, they were grateful that, although they had been warned to look out for marauding Indians, or common thieves, they had not encountered either thus far. Their animals were holding up well because there was plenty of grass and water available along the way. Fortunately, August tended to be a dry month in New England and it had been just that so far, making the journey swifter and more comfortable. They hoped that the weather would continue to hold, thereby ensuring that most of the roads over which they must travel would be in good condition.

Although they had procured some smoked meat while in Bennington, they knew that they had to carefully ration their stores to ensure that they would not run out before reaching Willsborough. Fortunately, there were lots of wild berries along the roadside and the children loved getting out of the wagon to pick them, popping them into their mouths and savoring the sweet juice that often trickled down their chins. Periodically, a farmer whose land they passed by, would offer them some fresh vegetables since these were in abundance at this time of year, and occasionally they were offered a freshly killed chicken or duck. Lydia's stores of flour, saleratus, salt and sugar had held up well, so she had no problem filling hungry stomachs with the bread that she baked on the open fire at the roadsides where they stopped for the night. Best of all, the hens had finally gotten used to being bounced around in the wagon and were laying eggs with great regularity.

With the routines of travel well established, and the days disappearing like the hours on the face of a clock, George and Lydia began to find themselves spending more and more time thinking about the life that lay ahead of them in Willsborough. George was heartened that he had the security of knowing that he could look forward to gainful employment in a business that had great promise for the future. This relieved him of some of his basic anxieties. Lydia, however, was filled with apprehension for herself and her children. Would they have a habitable place to live? Would they have a bit of land upon which to have a garden, and perhaps even some fruit trees? Would it be a safe and healthy environment for her family? Would she be able to rebuild the close friendships that she had experienced in Canaan? After all, they were going to a place referred to as the "wilderness" and that was enough to strike fear in one's heart.

As they came into Manchester, George noticed that the wagon had developed a bit of a wobble. Upon investigation, he discovered that the axle on one of the wheels had become dangerously loose. He hailed a passerby and asked where he might find a wheelwright and, fortunately, he was quickly guided to a shop just down the road. When the wheelwright heard of the journey that the family had made thus far, and learned how much further they had to go, he willingly set his work aside to assist them. Lydia and the children all piled out of the wagon, and even the chickens were lifted out in their coop. Needless to say, the birds were quite stunned by the bright light of the outdoors, which they had not seen for some time, and this set them off into a frenzy of squawking even more noisily than usual. With George assisting the wheelwright at the forge, the necessary repairs were done with dispatch, and after a night by the roadside, once again they were soon on their way.

They quickly passed through Dorset and Pawlet. Their goal was to reach the little town of Wells and to spend the night there just as they had done before. As the day began to wane

they found a quiet spot not too far off the roadway and settled down for the night. It seemed like in no time at all the cock was crowing lustily in an attempt to rouse them from their slumbers. With the usual quick breakfast behind them they were on their way still further north to just beyond Castleton where they had been told that there was a small lake just beyond where they could relax, perhaps even for a day if the weather was good. Fair winds prevailed, and the children delighted in being able to walk freely along the shore. It was just what they all needed. Alas, all too quickly it was time to move on.

Their next destination was Orwell, which they reached easily in a day. There they were told that they were not far from Lake Champlain. George learned that many ferries crossed Lake Champlain at various places.[44] He had had no idea that the lake was so vast and was like a highway all year around. He was told that for most of the year, boats plied their way back and forth across the water and, even in winter, the ice made a different type of highway. He heard that at Chimney Point there were two ferries that crossed to New York, one straight across to Fort St. Frederic and the other further north to Port Henry, and that at Addison there was a ferry across to Barber's Point, just below Westport. However, he was warned that if he chose the Barber's Point ferry, he would then have to travel north over a very rough and dangerous road that passed along the side of Split Rock Mountain. This was an area that was notorious for its rattlesnakes, fishers, mountain lions, and other hazards to a traveler. With this information in hand, George decided to continue his northerly progression along the east shore of Lake Champlain.

Before leaving on his journey, he had learned about a crossing that went from Charlotte, Vermont to a small settlement in the southern part of Willsborough. Charles McNeil, a former resident of Canaan, had established this ferry in 1790 and continued to operate it. George had not seen Charles since the latter had left Canaan and headed north some years earlier, and he had written a letter of inquiry to

Charles prior to his departure from Canaan. Charles had responded in a timely manner and assured George that he, his family, animals and goods could make a safe crossing to the the New York shore. Charles told George that, as an added benefit to those taking his ferry, in 1790 Platt Rogers had constructed a relatively flat road northward into the Village of Willsborough for his passengers.[45] With this knowledge, George derived great comfort that making the decision to continue northward was definitely for the best.

With the prospect of their journey's end coming closer and closer, George and Lydia began to focus upon the life that lay before them. Their mile-upon-mile trek had given them plenty of time to swing between excitement about their new life and fear of the unknown that lay ahead. They had been gone from home for almost three weeks. While they had been subjected to some rough roads that jogged their bodies and minds they had made the journey without serious accident or loss, or even serious illness of a child. Eldest child, Polly, had prided herself in playing the big sister role with young Orrin and George who needed much amusement as the long days passed. She seemed to always be able to devise a new game, a new song, and a new diversion. Much to George and Lydia's relief, baby Sally was an easy child, being quite content to nurse at her mother's breast and settle into the almost monotonous routine of the swinging and swaying of the wagon.

Although weary, these young parents knew that they had much for which to be grateful. Aside from the family, their team and horse, and even the ever-cranky chickens, they were continuing to make the trip safely and were physically fit except for being a bit on the thin side. The wheels, axles and other parts of the wagon had suffered some minor damage which had demanded repairs but, other than having the wagon threaten to tip over on a particularly bad stretch of road, they had had very few problems. They had climbed steep hills and forded some rushing streams exceptionally well. They were always fearful that their provisions would be exhausted before they got to the next place where they could restock, but that had not happened. Even finding water that looked pure enough to drink, although it might not look or smell wonderful, was an adventure. All along the way they found native plants bearing delicious berries and, occasionally, they came upon an abandoned orchard that was giving forth very tasty fresh fruit. They thanked God that fair weather and nature's bounty had treated them so well. Now, with a deep sigh of relief, they believed that at last they were soon to reach their ultimate destination. For now, they put all fears and worries aside, and relished the notion that their long journey was finally nearing an end.

LAKE CHAMPLAIN AT LAST

Once George had made a final decision regarding the best place for them to cross Lake Champlain, and they were on their way to Charlotte, he and Lydia really began to feel that the end of their long journey was within sight. The renewed vigor and determination that came with this allowed George to decide to pick up the pace a bit. However, having spent some time in Orwell assuring himself that he should proceed further north and check out each possible crossing along the way, he thought it prudent to make their trip to Shoreham a bit shorter than other days, and then try for somewhat longer days for the rest of their travels. This proved to be a wise decision because, several miles before they completed the nine-mile trek to Shoreham, it began to rain very hard.

Having seen the impending storm coming, with its ominous dark gray clouds and occasional claps of thunder, but no lightning, in the distance, George decided to seek shelter in a dense forest that lay alongside the road. Fortunately, a path into the woods had been cut by men who had timbered a portion of the forest fairly recently. He followed it just a little way and found a fine dense canopy of tall pines under which to park the wagon and tie up the animals. Although he knew that there was always the possibility that one of these trees could be struck by lightning, he decided to take that chance rather than subjecting his family and livestock to waiting out the storm in the open.

Lydia had a store of foods that did not need to be cooked and could be eaten in the wagon. As they huddled together to eat their evening meal under the protection of the canvas wagon top, they kept hearing rolls of thunder and seeing flashes of lightning that were able to penetrate even this dense wood. Mercifully, none came to where they were. They thanked God that they had endured so few adverse weather conditions on their journey. By nightfall, the storm had abated, and the stars showed their rain-swept brilliance against a crystal-clear sky.

As Lydia prepared her family for their night's repose, George got down from the wagon to see how his livestock had fared during the tumultuous downpour. Although he knew that animals were often terrified by a storm such as this one, George was immensely relieved to see that they had weathered it well. Since there was no place for them to graze in these woods, he fed them some of the hay that he always kept for just such occasions, and he patted them gently, reassuring them that all was well with their world once again. Fortunately, although the forest floor was damp, there had been no flooding because the storm had come through so quickly. Feeling reassured that all was well, a weary George climbed into the wagon and lay down to rest beside Lydia and baby Sally. The feather bed they had brought with them never felt so soft.

As the first rays of sunlight made their way through the dense forest, the rooster crowed lustily right on cue and dutifully roused his harem of hens, as well as his human family from their slumbers. Their morning repast accomplished, and the animals having been cared for, George yoked his oxen and mounted his horse for the day's thirteen-mile journey through Shoreham and on to Bridport. Fortunately, the road had been designed well so that much of the rainwater had rushed into the gullies alongside it. This made the going much easier for them. They were following a well-travelled route and were happy to pass occasional small farm houses along the way. There was something reassuring and comforting about seeing dwellings with chimneys sending forth wisps of smoke into the sky, and to smell the aroma of new-mown hay wafting through the air. As they traveled along they delighted in hearing the merry voices of small children at play under their mother's watchful eye and seeing farmers and their families going about their daily round of chores. It reminded them so much of home. As they fell asleep that night both Lydia and George tried to imagine what their new life would be like. George was certain that he would miss farming, which was all that he had ever known, and Lydia was keenly aware that she would have some lonely moments when she thought of the family and friends that she had left behind.

The next day's fifteen-mile journey took them through Addison where he heard about a ferry that made the short crossing from near Vergennes at Basin Harbor to Grog Harbor north of Westport. However, he was reminded of the hazards along the Split Rock Mountain chain that he had been told of before. Once again, he felt assured that crossing the lake north of this impediment was the wiser course of action. Proceeding to Charlotte, where his acquaintance Charles McNeil would take him across the lake to the road that would lead him into Willsborough, was definitely the best decision.

After a good night near Addison, they were underway once again and headed for Vergennes where they intended to settle for the night. The weather had remained clear which meant that they could follow their usual evening routine. The fifteen-mile trip that day had been tedious for everyone, and the children particularly were filled with pent up energy that they needed to rid themselves of. Since the surrounding land was relatively clear, and Otter Creek which flowed out to Lake Champlain was a mile or so further ahead, this seemed to be a safe place to let the children play on their own, but within sight of their mother. It was good for them to have the freedom to run and play while Lydia worked on the meal that she was preparing over the fire that George had laid, and George tended to his usual evening chores.

Early the next morning, they passed through the village and noted that, because it was on Otter Creek, Vergennes had the usual grist mill, sawmill, tannery, and blacksmith shop. There was also a potashery where potash was made for soap and glass, to process wool and flax, and provide fertilizer, along with the several inns and taverns that existed in most villages of any size.[46] George had decided to make the next day's journey from Vergennes through Ferrisburgh and into North Ferrisburgh a shorter day than usual. They all simply needed some time to catch their breath before the final leg of their long journey was truly upon them. Even the oxen and the horse seemed to appreciate this day of quiet reflection and the occupants of the coop were a bit calmer than usual.

The following day would take them into Charlotte and they wanted to be sure to arrive there early enough to spend the remainder of the day with ferry owner, and captain, Charles McNeil and his family. They found it hard to believe that this was the last night that they would be spending on the road. Over these past weeks they had become so completely in tune with the routines of the days on the road that they suspected there might be a bit of a void until they adjusted to their new way of life. As they went through the day that seemed to be much like any other Lydia and George found themselves balancing apprehension and relief. Yes, their journey would be over but what would their new life be like? They simply had no idea. George hoped that Charles would be able to tell him more about Willsborough than he already knew.

JOURNEY'S END

With the all-too-familiar morning routines accomplished in Vergennes, they set forth once again and, by midday, they had covered the five miles between North Ferrisburgh and Charlotte. As they crested the hill and came down to the ferry landing in little Charlotte Harbor, they got their first real view of Lake Champlain. Although they had caught glimpses of it here and there when they were on terrain that was high enough to allow them to see over the trees to the west, they had had little opportunity to visualize the expanse of water that lay between Vermont and New York. Because the day was somewhat overcast, they could not see across the lake to the opposite shore. Nevertheless, what they did see seemed like a vast expanse of unending openness.

As they pulled up to the ferry captain's house, Charles' wife, Thankful, and their children came running out to greet them. She had been keeping a watchful eye for their arrival for some days and was so relieved to see them at her doorstep at last. She explained that Charles was out on his boat taking some passengers and livestock across to the sandy landing beach to the south of the little settlement in Willsborough, and bringing others back to Charlotte. She reached out to help Lydia out of the wagon while taking the baby into her arms.

Sally seemed to be quite content to be held by anyone – even someone she had never seen before. Together, the two women walked into the McNeil's simple, but very serviceable, home that was situated just up from the water a bit, so that any high waves that might occur in a winter storm would do no harm to the house. Meanwhile, the Clark and McNeil children, some of whom were almost the same age, seemed to become comfortable with one another quite quickly, and soon they began running and gleefully chattering excitedly between themselves. Thankful told them that they were free to play outside as long as they stayed away from the water and were within sight. They scampered off happily. While Lydia cared for her baby and helped Thankful make the final preparations for the midday meal, George took care of securing the wagon and seeing that his horse and oxen were given water and taken to a place where they could graze.

Soon, Charles' sail ferry came into view in the harbor, and George went down to lend him a hand as he unloaded his few passengers and their animals. Although they had not seen one another since Charles left Canaan ten years before, they quickly embraced one another and began to reminisce about their mutual birthplace as Charles helped George take care of his ferry on land. With chores done, and the midday repast awaiting, George and Charles gathered up the happily playing children and went inside. The two families sat down together at the long trestle table, laden with food that stretched before them. After the slim rations on which the Clark family had been surviving, this looked like a true feast. Before they began to eat, they all bowed their heads in prayer, which included a special expression of gratitude that George and Lydia's journey had gone well, and that they were all together on this day. Soon, everyone was eating with great gusto. The children continued their conversations while their parents began reminiscing about Canaan. How quickly the adults made the interceding years, since the McNeil's had moved north to Charlotte, seem like yesterday.

When they had finished dining, the children ran outside to play once again, while Lydia and Thankful chatted happily as they did their chores. George went out to help Charles with his afternoon chores. Before long, it was time for Charles to secure his boat for the night. George helped him with this and then went up to make certain that his animals were safe. They had planned for George and his family to make an early morning departure across the lake if the weather remained fair. As dusk approached, the two families gathered for tea and a final bit of conversation. Afterwards, George and Lydia climbed back into their wagon for what might be their last night of sleep in their makeshift home away from home. Knowing that everything and everyone was truly secure gave George enormous peace of mind.

As soon as the first light of dawn came over the hill behind them, the Clark family members were wide awake and filled with excitement. This was the big day! They were going to cross the lake, and soon thereafter would arrive at their final destination, and the end of their almost month-long journey. Everyone quickly donned their clothes, and soon Lydia and the children were on their way back to the McNeil's house where they had been promised a special breakfast before their voyage to New York. The day was fair and as Lydia and her brood walked toward the house she looked to the west and was much relieved to see land on the other side of the lake where she had only seen a vast expanse of nothingness the day before. The entry door to the McNeil's house was flung open and they could smell delicious aromas wafting through the air. Meanwhile, George went down to the waterfront to help Charles prepare his sail ferry for the lake crossing, and to get his animals and wagon ready for the journey.

With this accomplished, the men went up to the house to join their families. The long trestle table was heaped with sausages and bacon, fresh eggs, apples, blueberries, homemade bread, butter and strawberry jam - all of which were the bounty of the McNeil's land. After their slim rations on the road, the Clark children's eyes fairly bulged as they saw a morning repast of such proportions. There was much to talk about as Charles endeavored to explain what their journey across the lake on the ferry would be like. He wanted to reassure them that they, their wagon, and their animals would arrive safely on the other side of what had seemed to them like an endless sea the day before. As the weather was good and she could see land on the other side of the lake Lydia was a bit relieved.

With their sumptuous breakfast completed, everyone walked down to the boat. Lydia was still feeling very

apprehensive about their journey across such a broad expanse
of water and was clutching Sally very close to her. Thankful,
who had made the crossing with her husband many times, did
her best to provide the reassurance that Lydia needed so
badly. Meanwhile, the children did not seem to be fazed by
this approaching adventure and could not wait to get on the
boat and on their way. As they got to the water's edge,
Charles was joined by a young boy who provided him with
assistance with his boat when he needed it.

Everyone gathered around the boat while Charles
explained that his ferry had a very flat bottom so that it could
be run right up onto the shore. He noted that this was what he
had to do in both Charlotte Harbor and on the other side of
the lake where the landing for Willsborough lay. Most of the
landings on Lake Chaplain were rocky. Fortunately, both of
his landing places had sandy beaches which was a great
advantage.

The ferry's floor was made of sturdy oak planks, and at
either end of the boat there was a wooden ramp that Charles
lowered to the shore to allow his passengers, their vehicles
and their livestock to get on and off easily. He pointed out that
his single sail was attached to a tall, strong pine mast that was
mounted to the right side of the gunnels that ran along both
sides of the boat. On top of the gunnel, there was a railing that
could be used to tie up livestock and cargo for the journey, or
for passengers to hold onto, if needed. George asked about the
long pole that was attached at the rear of the gunnel on the
sail side. Charles explained that this worked like a tiller, and
by moving this pole back and forth he could steer his vessel to
catch the best wind in his sails and move the boat forward on
a relatively even keel. He assured George that, as they sailed,
he would get a better understanding of how all of this worked.
However, for now Charles needed to get his passengers,
livestock and the wagon loaded on board. [47]

As they prepared to load the boat, Charles explained that
he needed to be careful to balance his vessel as evenly as
possible. For this reason, he wanted to board the horse first so

that he could keep the greater weight of the oxen and wagon in the middle of the boat. George had already saddled his steed and had him ready for boarding. He took him gently by his halter and led him from the tree to which he had been tied to the water's edge. As the horse got closer to the water, he started to balk a bit. However, with George in front of him holding a carrot a short distance from his nose, and Charles pushing gently from the rear, they were able to get him on board and safely tied to the gunnel rail on the left side of the vessel. Next, they loaded the oxen and wagon that George already had attached behind his team. As he started to move them toward the boat, he was grateful that these amazing beasts of burden were always so calm and steadfast, even through the most trying circumstances. They remained docile as he led them up the ramp and seemed unfazed by the fact that their hooves were not touching the familiar earth. He tied his team to the gunnel railing a safe distance behind his horse, just in case his steed got nervous and tried to kick what was behind him.

Now, it was time for Lydia and the children to go up the ramp and settle on the bench for passengers that lay at the rear of the left gunnel just opposite where Charles would be steering. With this accomplished, Charles hoisted the ramp up with the help of his boy, picked up the sturdy pole that he kept beside him, and pushed off the shore. He caught a gentle breeze that quickly filled his sail. The waters were relatively calm at this early hour in the day, for which Lydia and George were grateful. Knowing how anxious Lydia was, George stayed close to her for a bit just to reassure her. The children, however, thought that this was a wonderful adventure and were totally unfazed. As the boat began to rock gently to and fro, they quickly learned to sway with its pitches in order to keep their balance. With the wind in their faces, their expressions were those of pure joy and excitement. They were underway!

As they set forth on the broad lake, Lydia and George were awe struck by what lay before them. For the first time, they could see to the north and to the south where the water just seemed to keep going and going forever. This stretch of water was even more vast than they had ever imagined. Whether they looked to the north, south or straight ahead they saw a vast blue expanse, punctuated by occasional ripples as a gust of wind caught the water's surface. When they lifted their eyes from the watery blue they saw before them, range upon range of huge mountains ranked behind one another in a seemingly endless progression. From this perspective, they looked so much more rugged and impressive than the Berkshires back home. Despite their incredible beauty, George couldn't help thinking that there was a slightly brooding, and even somewhat sinister, quality to them, and he was glad that he was seeing these giants in the bright light of early morning sunshine.

Charles pointed out a small island to their north and told them the local story of this tiny piece of land. He explained that it was often referred to as Sloop Island. Purportedly, it got its name because during the Revolutionary War the British saw it rise out of the fog that enveloped the lake, whereupon they fired a barrage of cannonballs into what they mistook for a rebel ship. They gleefully thought that they had sunk the vessel ahead. Much to their surprise, when the fog lifted in the morning, they saw that it was only a tiny island. They must have been much chagrined.

As they moved closer to the New York shore, George noticed to the south what looked like a large peninsula, with a mountain rising steeply just a short distance from the water's edge. A little further, he could see a cleft in the rock face of the peninsula through which one could probably pass with a small boat. As it came into view more sharply, Charles explained that the peninsula with the cleft rock was actually called Split Rock, and the mountain that rose behind it went by the same name. Although he had never gone there on land, Charles said that he had been told by others that one must be wary of the vast number of rattlesnakes that inhabited the area. As George viewed the mountain, he was reminded of the reason that he had been advised not to cross the lake further south and travel through the Split Rock Mountain Forest. Seeing it, and hearing that there were rattlesnakes, in addition to all of the other wild beasts that lived there, simply strengthened his gratitude that he had not chosen the route that would have taken him there.

When they neared the western shore, on what had turned out to be a very tranquil crossing, even Lydia relaxed a bit and began to take in the sights before her. Before long, Charles pointed to a small group of buildings that huddled around the shallow bay before them. He explained that this settlement was in the southern portion of Willsborough, and noted that he had heard some talk from people that lived there that these settlers wanted to split their area away from Willsborough in order to become a hamlet of their own. He noted that nothing had happened thus far. As they came in still closer to shore, he pointed out a small beach and said that this was where he would be bringing in the ferry. The beach was quite sandy, and it provided a perfect place for a boat landing. He explained to his passengers that he would ask Lydia and the children to step ashore after he had lowered his sail, and then lowered the ramp. Then, when his passengers were safely on land, he would ask George for his assistance with getting his horse, and his oxen and wagon off.

Soon, as the ramp rumbled down to meet the soft beach, the children scampered ahead to the dry land that lay before them, and Lydia, with baby Sally in her arms, was close behind. Then, George approached his horse gently, and let the anxious animal nuzzle his open hand with his wet muzzle in search of the wisp of hay that George held for him. His steed sensed that something was going to happen, and his feet began to dance in anticipation as he eagerly stepped forward onto the ramp and then onto the beach which felt strange, but somehow warm and welcoming.

Next, George approached his team of oxen. They too had begun to paw the boat's floor a little as they felt the excitement of the moment. It took little coaxing to have them step off the boat, pulling the wagon behind them. With everyone safely on land, Charles left his beached boat briefly and led them up the gentle slope, and onto the road to Willsborough. He noted that the road would hug the shoreline until it reached the place where the Boquet River meets Lake Champlain. From there, it would cut inland before descending into the village, which lay in a valley between to large hills. He assured them that this would take them straight north to the village. As they bade a fond farewell, and Charles went back to his boat, the little family was suddenly overwhelmed by the fact that they had reached New York, their new home state. More importantly, in just a few miles their month-long journey would truly come to an end. They were a bit anxious but also very eager to reach their destination.

A NEW LIFE BEGINS

As soon as they stepped off Charles McNeil's sail ferry, and onto the shores of New York State, Lydia and George felt a lightness of heart that had not been present since they left Canaan. Seeing this excitement, the horse fairly pranced. Even the oxen seemed to sense that, after mile upon mile of trudging ahead, their long haul was coming to an end. There was a certain spring in their step. George found the road to the north as good as Charles McNeil had promised. It was well-traveled, with only an occasional rut or a fallen tree branch along the way. This last leg of their journey went very fast, and soon the road swerved sharply to the right as it descended a steep hill down to the banks of the Boquet River and into the Village of Willsborough. The rather precipitous hills that rose to the east and to the west of the river seemed to enfold the valley and the village. With their excitement becoming boundless, Polly, Orrin and George clambered to get down from the wagon to join their father and walk along beside him. As he lifted them down to the ground, he gave each of them a special hug.

Levi had sent George a letter prior to their leaving Canaan in which he told him that a simple log dwelling and a few simple pieces of furniture awaited them. He instructed him to come to the ironworks immediately upon arrival. In search of these, George guided his wagon along the river, first passing the bridge, and then moving on toward the wing dam that augmented the natural falls a short distance downstream. There he got his first glimpse of Willsborough's fledgling industrial site – the Anchor Shop. He assumed that it occupied this spot because of the opportunities offered by the abundance and forcefulness of the water that passed over the dam. As he neared the complex of buildings that had been constructed for the manufacture of anchors, George spotted his old friend Levi. Although some years had passed since they had shared their childhoods together in Canaan, they recognized one another instantly. Pleasantries were exchanged, and then Levi suggested that he lead them to their new home. Lydia was delighted at this prospect. Although she was happy about her husband's new employment, and happier still that their journey had finally ended, she was eager to see her new home and to go about the business of setting up housekeeping once again.

While George walked along, leading his horse so that he and Levi could chat, Lydia and Sally rode in the wagon. The two little boys and big sister Polly simply scampered along beside them. They were eagerly looking at the things that surrounded them, delighting in being able to run free at long last. Levi took the opportunity to describe Willsborough. He proudly stated that according to the 1800 Federal Census that had been taken just the year before, the village and its environs now boasted a population of 212 householders and 1,802 inhabitants.[48] Levi pointed out the sawmill, as well as the buildings along the riverbank that housed some of the tradesmen including a blacksmith, wheelwright and a harness maker. These further contributed to the success of the village. Once past the bridge, they started up the hillside where there were a few simple frame houses.

Levi noted that many of these were occupied by those who were employed at the anchor works, sawmill, and gristmill. Since for most of the tradesmen, their home and workplace were one, they tended to settle down on the road by the river. At the top of the hill the land flattened out and allowed space upon which to construct houses and the necessary outbuildings, and to create a small barnyard, and a garden plot for each dwelling. There, Levi proudly pointed out a house with its door flung open as if to reach out and beckon them to come forward. He told George that this was the house that had just been built for them. As Lydia stepped down from the wagon and viewed her new home she gave a sigh of relief and her former apprehensiveness gave way to a more cheerful demeanor. Levi pointed out that his own house was very close by. After their long journey that had taken them all so far from the small towns in the Berkshires that they had always known, it was reassuring to Lydia that they would be close to the Higby family.

As they neared the house Levi's wife, Chloe, came through the doorway and fairly ran toward them with a wreath of smiles lighting up her countenance. Lydia and Chloe embraced one another with tears faintly welling up in their eyes. The bond that they had formed in the years before Levi and Chloe had moved on to Fort Ann was quickly reestablished amid the chatter and excitement of the occasion. The Higby children, Alanson and Levi, Jr., who were close to the ages of the older Clark children, came clambering out the door through which their mother had just exited, bursting with excitement about meeting new friends. There was a mad rush of introductions and greetings by all as Chloe picked up each of George and Lydia's children in turn and gave them a special welcoming hug. Then she turned back to Lydia who was clutching baby Sally and gently took the baby into her own arms and began to rock and sing to her. Sally opened her eyes briefly and shone a radiant smile.

With a cheery goodbye Levi returned to his Anchor Shop after assuring George that he understood that his most pressing need had to be to see that his family was comfortably settled. He promised him that he did not expect him to officially begin work until the end of the week. George and his family quickly waved good-bye to him and walked into their new home. Chloe knew that Lydia and George needed time together to take in all that lay before them, so she took Orrin and George by the hand, with Polly and her own children following, and headed down the road toward her house. With a quick, light step, and a wreath of smiles on their faces, George and Lydia embraced one another tenderly and began their new lives as citizens of Willsborough. The anguish and travails of the long journey north began to silently slip away, and hope for a brighter and better life for himself and his family enveloped George.

It seemed that Levi and Chloe had thought of everything to make the Clarks feel welcome and cared for. Chloe had swept and cleaned the house, and even had a cheery fire blazing on the hearth. In front of it was a trestle table and around it were enough simple straight chairs to accommodate them. There were no other real furnishings, and so they would have to provide everything else they needed as time permitted. However, this was enough for now. On the table, Chloe had laid bunches of carrots and onions from her garden, a hunk of salted pork, a freshly baked loaf of bread and some sweet-smelling butter. This was enough to get them started, especially since there were still a few foodstuffs left in the wagon.

While Lydia sat down to tend to her little one, George went out to fetch his team and his horse that were tethered to a nearby tree. He led them gently to a small enclosure behind the house. There, he removed the yoke that had been placed on the necks of the oxen day after day during the journey. They shook their heads as if to make sure that it was really gone, and they were free to act independently. Then, he turned to his faithful steed who was waiting patiently to be relieved of his saddle and reins and to be rid of the bit in his mouth. In no time, the animals quickly discovered the small pile of fresh hay that lay in one corner and began nuzzling around in it with delight. As Levi turned, he noted that Chloe had brought some buckets of water and that would meet the immediate needs of the animals had been carried up from the river. He brought one forward for the animals to see and left it there for them to drink when they were ready. Suddenly, there was a great deal of squawking coming from the wagon that was still parked by the front door of the house. The hens and the rooster were protesting that they had been forgotten. Because the travel coop was too heavy to lift with the birds in it, George decided to take them to the enclosure one by one. After he had gotten them all there, he went back for the coop which he placed in a corner not far away from the water buckets. This would be the nighttime residence of his poultry that would protect them from prowling wild animals.

This accomplished, George began unloading the wagon. As he lifted out each item, Lydia almost wept for joy. Her rocking chair, the baby's cradle, a handsome mantel clock that had been in her family for some years, the beautiful quilts that she had made during the long winter evenings at her old home, and the family Bible with all of her family's records came out first. Next came the pots and pans, cooking utensils, cutlery and plates that Lydia would need to prepare the evening's meal. Only the essentials could be unpacked right away. The rest would have to wait for another day as evening was fast approaching. As George and Lydia worked cheerfully alongside one another, he sensed that Lydia's senses were definitely less ragged as she saw these familiar things in their new setting.

Although it would take weeks, and even perhaps months, to become completely settled Lydia and George made sure that things were taken care of enough to remind the children of their home in New Marlborough and Canaan, and make them feel more comfortable in their present surroundings. Even a few familiar toys were lying on the floor beside the hearth. Baby Sally was cooing happily in the cradle, feeling well sated from her mother's milk, and reveling in the warmth that surrounded her and the cradle's gentle rocking. With all in order for now, George walked along the hilltop toward the Higby house to pick up the children and bring them home. There, he found Polly contentedly following Chloe around as Orrin and George happily played with their newfound friends. Although they were reluctant to leave, George whisked his children away with promises of a return visit the very next day. The children skipped along beside their father eagerly sharing the excitement of their new friendships and their enthusiasm for their surroundings.

As the children came through the door into their new home, they were delighted by the aroma that wafted through the air. The sights and smells before them reminded them so much of their former home. With food on the table from the wagon and Chloe's stores the little family gathered in prayer. They thanked God for the bounty before them, as well as their safe arrival and warm welcome in Willsborough. Everyone ate gustily - almost as if they had not had a bite to eat on their journey. While George went out to the enclosure to check on his animals and make certain that they would be alright for the night, Lydia went about the task of washing up after the evening's meal while Polly, in her usual manner, kept the younger children amused.

George had explained to his family that, since they had no bedsteads as yet, the most comfortable place to sleep would be back in the wagon. As much as spending the night in their new home would have been a wonderful treat, the children seemed quite content to crawl back into the beds they had made for themselves and slept in for so long. It took no time for everyone to be fast asleep. Even George was able to bask in the glory of an unworried night's sleep knowing that his animals were safely ensconced in the little enclosure. It had been a long and intensely exciting day for everyone.

Lydia and George awakened early the next morning. The children were all still fast asleep, except, of course, for baby Sally who was totally in tune with her mother's doings. They quietly climbed out of the wagon and headed back into the house. Once George had seen that Lydia and the baby were settled in the kitchen he went out to the enclosure to see how his animals had fared. The rooster crowed with gusto as the hens continued pecking away at the earth. They had even laid a few eggs. This was their way of saying thank you for getting us out of that coop where we were constantly tossed around as if we were mere balls. The oxen shambled over to greet George and bowed their heads in search of a treat. Instead, they got a scratch on their muzzles. Soon his horse came along for the same attention. George emptied a pail of water into a bucket for them and they lined up to take their turns sucking in huge gulps of the refreshing liquid.

Knowing that all was well in the barnyard, George retraced his steps back to the cabin. As he entered the door he could tell that Lydia had wasted no time getting her fire going and preparing the morning's meal. When all was ready George went over to the wagon to awaken the children. Polly was already up and dressed and was helping little George put on his clothes. Meanwhile, she and Orrin chattered steadily about the day's plans to play with Alanson and Levi again. They jumped out of the wagon, and in no time they had had their morning repast and were ready to walk the short distance to Levi and Chloe's house. George watched them from the doorway for a moment just to be sure that they got to their destination safely, and then turned back into the house to see if Lydia needed any help. After he had done as much as he could to be of assistance he decided to walk down into the village. He wanted to get to know it a bit before he started his regular work at the Anchor Shop.

As George walked along the river, he could not help thinking about how much there was to see and learn, and it was all so different from what they had left behind in Canaan and New Marlborough. Although there were climatic similarities, Levi had told him that the presence of such a large body of water, that was usually frozen over for several months each year, had a significant impact upon the way of life of those living near it. Winters were longer because the water was still so cold from the ice and, as a result, farmers could not begin to work the soil until late spring. The reverse happened in the autumn when the warmer lake extended the harvest season. With this in mind, George was beginning to see that, although it appeared that some things were the same as what he knew, there were definitely vast differences. Even though he was no longer a farmer, he realized that this would impact the way in which he went about using his small plot of land. Since it was far too late for him to do anything now, he hoped that he could depend upon those who had worked the land for an entire season to share any surplus food for him as his family, as well as for his livestock. He was certainly ready to offer help with the harvest in return.

George was very certain that he would face many challenges in the months ahead as he learned how to do new tasks in a new workplace, built a permanent structure to house his livestock, erected more solid fences around the enclosure, built some simple furniture, helped others in return for goods, and spent at least a little time with his family. He would be very busy indeed! As he walked up the hill toward his home, he could see that the Higby and Clark children were happily engaged as Alanson and Levi Jr. hastened to introduce their new friends to the surrounding fields and woods, and also to some of the neighboring children. George couldn't help marveling at the way in which young children could form bonds with such ease, when it was so much harder for adults. He was very happy for his offspring that the transition to Willsborough seemed to be going so well in just two days.

As he reached the top of the hill, and neared the door of his new home he saw that Chloe was with Lydia once again. She greeted George fondly and said that she had come to lend a hand where it was needed most. For Lydia, the biggest help Chloe could give was to care for baby Sally so that her mother could have the much-needed time to finish the job of unpacking and sorting. As Chloe played with Sally, and Lydia went about her chores, the two happily engaged in conversation about their old homes, and friends and relatives in Canaan. Chloe was truly delighted to hear that things remained largely as they had been when she and Levi lived there. At times, she missed Canaan, but she and Levi were very happy with their lives in Willsborough. The two women were amazed that the years since they had seen one another seemed almost like yesterday, and Lydia had so many questions to ask that she hardly knew where to begin, so they simply let the conversation flow as they became reacquainted.

As Chloe and Lydia chatted, Samuel Brown's wife, who lived right next door, came by with a freshly baked pie and an offer to be of assistance in any way she could. Very soon thereafter Levi Cooley's wife who lived next door on the other side, stopped in with several loaves of bread that she had just popped out of her oven.[49] Lydia was quite overwhelmed by the warmth and hospitality that her family was receiving from their new neighbors. Chloe told her that they had all gotten together before their arrival, and the women and men had figured out what each of them could do to make the transition of this new family as easy as possible. They wanted Lydia and George to know that their privacy would be respected, but that they were there to assist them in any way they could. Lydia sighed as she thought about how kind these strangers were and looked forward to their becoming good friends in the months to come. She was confident that soon she would feel a part of her new community.

It did not take long for Lydia to unpack the few pots, pans, dishes and cutlery that she had brought from home, as well as the foodstuffs that were still in the wagon. Until George had time to build a cupboard for her, she was quite content to keep things in the crates and boxes that had lined the sides of the wagon, and now had been moved into the house. With the help of the foodstuffs that Chloe had shared with her so generously, as well as the delicious smelling bread and pie that had just been delivered, she would provide a sumptuous noon dinner for her family.

When George came into the house, she asked him if he could prepare a fire for her since the one she had hastily laid in the early morning had gone out. He went out to the small pile of wood that had been carefully split and laid up for him by the neighbors and selected a bundle of nice dry hickory for the fire. He carried it in, placed it on the hearth, and began to lay the fire in just the way that Lydia liked. As he did so, he could not help thinking how happy it made him to see Lydia feeling more at ease. He looked forward to seeing the glow on her cheeks as she went about the daily ritual of preparing food for her family.

As Lydia turned to tend to her fire, she realized that for today she would not be able to get the small oven in the side of her fireplace hot enough to bake and was glad for her neighbor's thoughtful offerings. However, as she went about her other tasks she thought about how much she was looking forward to baking her first loaf of bread in her new oven. It would certainly be easier that what she had dealt with along the road. She loved to make bread, mixing her special ingredients together, letting it rise in the pan that she covered with an old piece of linen, and then gently kneading the soft mass in her hands until it reached the perfect texture and shape to be popped into the oven. With the fire well in hand, George went back outside to take care of the never-ending need for a fresh supply of water for cooking, cleaning up, and for bathing too. He was happy that a bubbling spring lay not too far away from his house. He filled his buckets and took them into the house, and then left Lydia to go about her preparations while Chloe remained a bit longer to help with the baby.

Now, George needed to get to his outside chores. He knew that learning how to do his new job would be very tiring and time-consuming initially, and he realized that before he started work at the Anchor Shop, he must tackle at least some of the most important projects that awaited his attention. Taking care of the livestock that had come so far with him and making preparations to add other animals in the future, was critically important. He was grateful that his new neighbors had been kind enough to construct a rudimentary enclosure that would take care of his livestock until he could complete a more permanent structure that would protect them from the rigors of the wind, ice and snow that were yet to come. For now, George was especially concerned about his chickens because he had been told that wolves prowled around the little community at night and owls swept overhead searching for easy prey. They thought nothing of picking off any animal or bird that they could. He felt that for now the only recourse for his fowl was to put them in their travel coop and tie it down securely in the enclosure.

The knowledge that he had acquired on his farm in New Marlborough was invaluable as he planned the type of structure that would work best for his livestock and calculated the amount of wood he would need for that purpose. As he was thinking about all of this, one of his new neighbors came by and offered him the use of his sledge since George did not have one yet. This would greatly expedite dragging logs for the shelter from the woods to his temporary enclosure. Soon, George had hitched his team of oxen to the sledge and, with axe in hand, had set out to the nearby woods where he selected trees of the proper size and sturdiness for his purpose, and quickly and expertly felled them. He figured that, once he had accumulated enough rough timbers, he would turn to the task of cutting each piece to the proper size, and then notching the ends in preparation for assembling a sturdy log structure for his livestock.

As he moved along through the day's endeavor, George kept thinking about how much he enjoyed this type of the work. He realized that he would miss working outdoors all day when he was at the Anchor Shop. However, he was ready to learn something new. Today's task was especially enticing because it gave him the opportunity to explore a bit and learn about the land and forest that surrounded his home. He was glad to know that if he needed milled wood he would be able to take his timbers to the sawmill on the river for ripping, and he was very grateful that his new neighbors had already offered to help him with the construction project, if he needed assistance.

George thought about how eloquently this type of generosity spoke of the type of community that he had moved into. Although much of the day was consumed by this project, by dusk he had assembled quite a pile of freshly cut wood. George prided himself on thinking ahead and, while he worked on the shelter, he began to give some thought to the next task, once this one was completed. He knew that he would need to put up a more permanent type of fencing for his livestock, and he figured that he could use some of the smaller pieces of timber that he had recently felled to construct a rough-hewn zigzag fence that some referred to as a snake fence. This would be easier to construct than a straight fence because it would require no posts or hardware.

George hoped that during the months before the ground froze hard he would be able to begin to clear some of his small woods to create a pasture for his livestock and an area in which he could grow crops to feed them. He knew that Lydia was eager for a plot of land on which she could grow vegetables, as well as the herbs that were invaluable for medicinal, preservative and cooking purposes. Perhaps by next spring he would have accomplished this and even be able to establish an orchard like the one he had at home in New Marlborough. He was certain that he would need advice about which fruit trees would flourish in this climate. For now, George's challenge was to prioritize the many tasks that lay before him. He knew that it would be months, and even years, before he had completed all of his projects. He would simply have to tackle one thing at a time and be patient.

The time before George began his work at the Anchor Shop simply flew by as there was so much to do, and as the day before he would begin work neared he was relieved that he had been able to accomplish as much as he had. He had done enough on the shelter for his animals that, although not complete, it was functional, and the fence was already up. He knew that he would want to extend it later. At least, the immediate needs of his family and animals had been met. He was so happy to see that Lydia was quickly becoming content with her new home, and the children had already become thoroughly immersed in their new life with their new surroundings and friends. Already, memories of the arduous journey from Canaan were beginning to recede.

THE ANCHOR SHOP

With his family somewhat settled, George was eager to learn about his new job. Levi had suggested that he come for a tour before he actually began to work at the Anchor Shop. It was a beautiful late August day, and George decided that this was the day for his visit. As he walked along the river and watched the waters of the Boquet River wash under the bridge on their way to the lake, he had an opportunity to reflect upon the vast array of new impressions and experiences that were racing through his mind. As he passed the harness maker's shop, he was greeted warmly, and the blacksmith came out of his smithy door to wave a hand. It was clear that Levi had alerted these community members that the Clark family had arrived. Across the river, the sawmill was noisily attacking the boards that waited for attention just outside. The force of the river as it passed over the wing dam provided the source of power that this mill and the Anchor Shop needed to run their equipment. George's pace accelerated as his destination came into view.

Levi had suggested that George meet him at the pocket forges by the river and said that they would proceed from there. When he arrived, Levi came forward to greet him and hastened to introduce the other manager of the operation, George Throop. As the men exchanged formalities, George remembered Levi telling him about Throop, and the Throop-Higby friendship that had developed when both families were living in Fort Ann. He had said that when Charles Kane was seeking managers for his and Daniel Ross's venture in Willsborough he scouted for men who were skilled in working with iron. Fort Ann was a logical place to look because there was an active iron furnace where both Levi Higby and George Throop worked.

As part of their orientation for their new worker, Levi and George described the terms of the contract that Daniel Ross and Charles Kane had entered into with the fledgling U.S. Navy.[50] As managers, their job was to oversee every aspect of the Shop's operations and to ensure that the ten-year contract with the U.S. Navy was fulfilled to the satisfaction of the Anchor Shop's backers. This meant that there could be no impurities in the ore, or carelessness in the manufacturing process that would weaken the anchors they produced. The safety of the men on board the ships that carried these anchors was dependent upon the anchors' strength and durability. Both men said that they felt a considerable weight of responsibility and took their work very seriously. With pleasantries exchanged, Levi and George set off on their tour.

They began by climbing a rather steep hill set back from the river. While they walked, Levi explained the production cycle of the Anchor Shop. It operated at peak capacity when shipping overland, or on the lake, was possible. They had to stop production during the spring thaw which usually lasted throughout the month of April and well into May. During the thaw, the Boquet river became swollen with melting snow and ice from the mountains and streams to the west. Ice jams formed, and flooding was right behind these. During this period, trees and other debris came rolling through the village and over the dam. It was not safe to navigate the river, and the paths along the banks were made impassable because of the thick mud created by the melting snow and thawing earth. If it had been a particularly cold winter and the ice on the broad lake was very thick, it took a long time to melt and the cold water continued to delay the advent of spring.

As production slowed accordingly, the workers could turn to their own plots of land to begin preparing them for the crops that they would need to grow for their families and their livestock. When work at the Anchor Shop commenced once again, in late May or even early June, it was at a somewhat slower pace. Summer came quickly and soon the intense heat created by the furnace and the forges made working conditions difficult. In addition, the workers needed time to tend their crops and gardens in order to be prepared for the long winter that inevitably lay ahead. Now, with September approaching, and the heat beginning to abate, production was ramping up once again.

The weighing shed at the top of the hill was their tour destination. There, George saw barrels filled with different materials and a huge scale. John, a strong, burly man sporting an expansive leather apron that was covered with grime, stepped forward to greet them. He explained that, in his role as weighmaster, he was responsible for exactly measuring the charcoal used to ignite the fire in the furnace, the limestone that served as flux and removed impurities, and the iron ore that would be melted into pig iron by the intense heat of the fire in the furnace below. George watched the process intently as John's helpers loaded each carefully weighed ingredient into a barrow and pushed these downhill on a covered ramp that led to the bottom of the furnace. When they said goodbye to the weighmaster, Levi expressed his appreciation of John's diligence in seeing that this crucial stage was done to exact specifications.

As they walked down the ramp behind the barrows, George got to look at the furnace more carefully than when he had passed by it earlier. He asked why the furnace was built of stone rather than brick, and Levi explained that the particular type of limestone in the area was abundant and very durable, whereas brick had to be made and what was produced locally seemed to be rather soft. George noticed that the furnace was wide at the bottom and narrowed as it went up to which Levi responded that the sloping sides that culminated in a sort of chimney at the top, as well as the height, ensured maximum draw so that the fire would burn efficiently. When they reached the bottom of the furnace they saw the furnace master and his helpers hard at work as they unloaded the measured amounts of charcoal, limestone and iron ore from the weigh shed. Levi whispered that if the furnace master or his workers made any error in this process the final product would be weakened and made unusable, so their job was critically important. This was the reason that the furnace master could not stop to greet them.

George watched carefully as the furnace master laid twigs on the bottom of the furnace that would be used to ignite the charcoal placed above them. Soon after being lit, George could see that the coals were turning white hot and found himself instinctively stepping away from the intense heat as he saw one of the furnace master's helpers load in the limestone which would catch impurities. When the coals had become white hot again, another helper carefully shoveled in the iron ore while another manned huge leather bellows that forced air through a crude iron pipe and caused the fire to remain white hot throughout the process. Soon, George saw several men with long-handled sieves step forward to skim off the limestone slag, and then release the purer molten iron ore, which was commonly referred to as pig iron, into an area below the hearth. There, it flowed through a large funnel called a sow where the waiting workers would ladle the pig iron into wood molds called pigs. George was quite amused by all of this swine terminology.

At this point, Levi said that they needed to move along and would have to miss seeing the pigs broken out of the molds. They crossed the road to the pocket forges where they had begun the tour. George was eager to see this aspect of the operation because, at last, he would experience something that he could understand. Workers from the furnace had delivered several barrows of "pig" iron bars that needed to be reheated and turned into a pasty looking metal. Several men, beat the metal with heavy forge hammers, thereby driving off any excess carbon and impurities. The result of this refining process was bar iron which was then reheated and poured into the varying size anchor molds. [51]

George realized that he knew very little about anchors, and certainly had no idea of what anchors that could hold large seabourn ships in position looked like. Levi admitted that he, too, had had much to learn when he came to Willsborough. Fortunately, the Navy's specifications were very precise, and it was expected that these would be adhered to at all times. The size of the anchor being used was directly dependent upon the size of the vessel that would carry it. Many of the largest ships carried multiple different sizes of anchors depending upon the type of anchorage they would encounter. Levi pointed out that in their Anchor Shop they manufactured what were called long-shanked Admiralty anchors which were made in three parts: the shank that was a long, straight piece of iron with a crown or hooked piece at the end that would dig into the floor of the waterbody; the wood stock that was a crosspiece near the end of the shank; and, the iron ring that would be attached to a chain or rope. He added that if the manufacturing process had any defects the anchor could snap where the crown met the shank. At their Anchor Shop they were producing anchors that weighed 300 to 1,500 pounds and each of these required a special mold.[52]

Levi explained that he had several pressing matters to attend to and bade George farewell. With his mind filled with a dizzying array of thoughts regarding his future work, George bade goodbye to Levi and assured him that he would be at the Anchor Shop and ready to work in the morning. Fortunately, Levi had chosen to start George in the forges where he would feel more familiar, and then to move him gradually into various positions. Levi believed that George would learn quickly and hoped that he could move him along through the various aspects of the operation so that he could be a backup for him and George, should they need to be away from the Shop for some reason. Although he had so much to learn, George was confident that he would be adept at developing the skills required at the Anchor Shop and felt very appreciative that he had been given the opportunity to work there.

The very next day, George arrived at the Anchor Shop with eagerness, but yet a bit of trepidation. He prayed that he had not put his young family through so much in vein, and that he would be successful. His first day was very busy and challenging, and the time simply flew by. It felt good to pick up familiar tools at the forge to which he was assigned, and to begin hammering at the pig iron that had come from the furnace until he was certain that there were no impurities and it was strong bar iron. When the day's work was coming to an end, he tamped down the fire in his forge and laid out the tools that he would need in the morrow.

As he walked along the river, he could not help thinking about how different his life and the lives of his wife and children were going to be. Farming was all that he had ever known and life on a farm was the only frame of reference for them. Canaan and New Marlborough were villages that they visited upon occasion, but living right in a village, rather than outside, was a new experience for them. Even though he was no longer a farmer, he realized that this experience would impact the way in which he went about using his small plot of land. Since it was far too late for him to do anything much with this plot before winter set in, he could only hope that he could depend upon those who had worked the land for an entire season before to share any surplus food with him and his family, as well as his livestock. He was certainly ready to offer help with the harvest in return and to barter in any other ways that he could.

The days sped by for George. He proved to be a quick learner and soon moved into the final position at the forges where the finishing touches were given to the anchors. As an anchor was completed and ready for shipment, he looked at it with pride. Even though the work could be routine, and even backbreaking at times, or discouraging when the piece did not come out as expected, he always found it interesting. He wondered how the finished anchors got to their final destination, and was glad that one day Levi had the time to tell him how they got from Willsborough to the Navy distribution center in West Troy.

Levi explained that there were two possible means of transportation. He said that in the warmer months, when the lake was not frozen, and the Boquet River was navigable after the spring thaw, the anchors were loaded onto one of Captain McCrea's lighters, either the *Lion* or the *Anchor Shop*, at the

Anchor Shop landing. He transported them down the river to Lake Champlain where they were put on an awaiting sloop that took them up the lake to Whitehall.[53] George queried Levi as to why he said that they were sent up Lake Champlain when the sloops were actually going south. That concept really puzzled him until Levi explained that the lake actually flows from south to north as it wends its way to the Richelieu River and then on into the St. Lawrence River. At Whitehall, the lake came to an end so the anchors had to be offloaded onto wagons whose drovers took them overland on a well-trodden path as far as Fort Edward where they could be transported south on the Hudson River to their final destination, West Troy.

Levi went on to add that there was a different mode of transport for at least four of the winter months when the lake was frozen solid and became a busy highway. From late December until sometime in mid-April, or occasionally later, teams of sturdy mules, that were shod with cleats to grip the ice, dragged huge sleds from the Anchor Shop down to a landing on the river where they were met by itinerant mule drivers. Depending upon the weight and size of the anchors teams of men then loaded them onto different types of sleds for the journey south. On the broad lake, the mule drivers followed a path that was marked by evergreens that had been stuck into the ice just before it froze solid. Once at Whitehall, the mules were driven overland to Fort Edward, dragging their sleds on the snow that had been packed down to create a type of roadway, and from there they completed their journey to West Troy over the frozen Hudson River.

George tried hard to imagine what either of these journeys south would be like. On the one hand, it sounded like a great adventure, but on the other it seemed a bit more dangerous than he wanted to contemplate. For now, he was very content to stay right in Willsborough.

WILLSBOROUGH IS HOME

George very quickly adapted to his new occupation and truly enjoyed his labors at the Anchor Shop. Throughout the winter months, when the shop was running at full capacity, he discovered that the work was physically very demanding and inherently dangerous, so one had to be watchful at every turn. As Levi had predicted, George was a fast learner and soon advanced from one work site to another. Although he continued to favor working at the forge where the newly formed anchors got their final finishing touches, he had acquired enough basic skills to step in almost anywhere that he was needed. This was of great benefit to Levi and his partner George Throop and both parties marveled at how fortunate they had been to reconnect with one another in this place that was so far from their common birthplace.

As he and Lydia had expected, the winter of 1801-1802 was a bit longer than at home in Canaan and New Marlborough, but mercifully everyone in the family remained healthy. Even the animals, including the fractious chickens, had managed well. As they had hoped, there had been an outpouring of support from community members who had provided them with the foodstuffs that they needed. Neighbors and friends had seen that there was always enough food on the table, as well as a sufficient supply for the animals. In return, as he had promised, George had worked hard to help others as they were bringing in their crops so this reciprocal relationship was of benefit to everyone. He and Lydia both continued to be amazed by the generosity and kindness that had been shown them and, as time went by, they had begun to adapt to their new surroundings and soon had settled into predictable routines.

George had developed a balance between work at the Anchor Shop and time at home. The first thing each morning, he gathered a nice load of wood from the trees that he had felled in the fall, and then split for firewood for Lydia's fireplace. He carefully ranked the logs just outside the door, and as much under the cabin's eaves as possible. (If it was raining or snowing he would bring a load inside to dry beside the fireplace.) Then, he went out to attend to his animals before coming in for the breakfast that Lydia had prepared for her family. With morning chores behind him, and a fine morning meal completed, George donned his heavy overcoat and hat and turned to kiss each member of his brood, while admonishing the children to be good and help their mother during his absence. Lydia and little Sally got special hugs. Then, taking in hand the slight midday repast that Lydia had packed for him, he headed down the hill and along the river to the Anchor Shop.

Like everyone in his community, his day's routine was aligned with the hours of daylight and darkness. As dusk settled in and the day's occupation at the Anchor Shop drew to a close, George, and his fellow workers, wended their way to their homes and their other responsibilities. He stepped into his home just long enough to grab a couple of buckets of water that he kept just inside the door so that their contents would not freeze. Then, without pulling off his sturdy boots, or the warm coat and hat that Lydia had made for him, he went straight to his evening chores, even sometimes in the teeth of a gale and raging snowstorm. This was simply his lot in life and he accepted it for what it was.

With gratitude, George thought of the faithful work of his horse and his yoke of oxen during their journey north. He loved to come up to them to rub their noses, scratch behind their ears, and feel their warm breath on him, especially on those cold winter mornings. He realized how dependent he was upon these powerful beasts of burden. George admired them so much because they seemed to understand his every word and gesture. He loved his faithful horse too and hoped that as time went by he would be fortunate enough to acquire a second horse to help him with the lighter chores, and to take him and his family to places that were beyond walking distance. For now, he was content with what he had.

As he reached his animal's small enclosure and their shed, he could hear the snort of his oxen, a gentle neigh from his horse and, or course, a squawk from his chickens who had already gone to bed and disliked the intrusion of their owner. He had to remind himself that everything in their lives, even hens laying eggs, was related directly to hours of daylight so bedtime came early for them. The oxen and horse got fresh water and a bit more hay to carry them through the night. Even though it would freeze quickly, he refilled the small water receptacle in the coop and pitched in a few morsels of corn which they chose to ignore, at least until he was out of sight.

When George returned to the cabin, he was greeted eagerly by his little brood as each of them vied to get the first hug of the evening. Little Sally had learned to stay out of the way of her older siblings and quietly waited her turn. As usual, Lydia was beside the fireplace where she was making the final preparations for the evening repast. She would have preferred to offer her larger meal of the day at midday as she had done back on the farm. However, that was not possible with George spending his days at the Anchor Shop and not wanting to leave the forge fire that he had built to perfection in order to come home at the midday repast. So, of necessity she and her children had adapted to the new routine.

With the evening meal taken care of, George made a brief trip back to his little barnyard to be sure that his animals were safely enclosed for the night. Meanwhile, Lydia, with the help of Polly, cleaned up the remains of their meal and then turned her attention to the final round of the day's activities. She took Sally onto her lap to nurse her and was glad that the babe was gradually beginning to wean herself. Lydia sang softly as Sally indulged in her mother's milk and soon her tiny eyes began to close. With that accomplished, Lydia gently laid her young one on the cot that lay right next to the bed that she and

George shared.

With his outdoor chores completely finished, George went back to the cabin and took his turn with the three older children. He gathered them together to say their prayers, and with a final amen, he helped them up the steep ladder to the loft above. Soon, Lydia joined them. She helped Polly to snuggle down under her covers and, as she did so, she was reminded, once again, of how much her eldest child did to be a helpful daughter. Meanwhile, George tried to get his sons to settle down. Sometimes this could be a very challenging process. Once this was accomplished and all three children were dozing off, their parents, with candles in hand, descended to prepare for their own evening's rest.

Sometimes, if fatigue had not completely overwhelmed her, Lydia would pull her rocker up close to the fire where the flickering light of her candle was enhanced by the light of the flames from the fireplace, while George did the few simple chores that he could without much light to see by. Soon, fatigue, and the thought that dawn would come all too soon, told George that he should bank the fire so that there might be a few embers in the morning. That done, they retired to their rough bedstead in the corner of the room and snuggled into the featherbed that they had brought all the way from Canaan. Yet another day had ended!

During those winter months, Lydia's life was just as busy as George's. From dawn to dusk, her days followed a sort of ritualistic pattern, that only varied with the time of year, illness or death. Winter days were especially long and lonely for her as she followed a set of monotonous routines day after day and had little opportunity to get out of her home to be with other women in her community. She was well aware that, of course her primary responsibility was to take care of her four children. Her day began at dawn when she arose to nurse Sally, and then turn to her morning routines. Polly was seven years old and, like most young girls, already understood that she was expected to help her mother with household chores and childcare. Sally, who was now almost a year old, was toddling around behind her mother and getting into anything that attracted her attention, at which point big sister Polly would be summoned for assistance. The boys, Orrin and George, were at an age where they were quite content to amuse themselves, and if the weather was fair they loved to go outside to tumble around in the leaves, or later, the snow, or walk a way to see their friends.

Lydia spent much of her day keeping the fire in the fireplace blazing in an effort to maintain some element of warmth within the walls of their cabin, as well as a place upon which to prepare meals for herself and her family. Early each morning, she arranged the wood that George had put out for her in just the proper way, took out the tinder box and started the fire she needed to cook the morning meal, and the other two meals to follow. During this time when they were so dependent upon others for food, the menu for each day was always a bit of surprise. Sometimes, it was a slab of smoked ham or bacon, or a joint of beef or even a bit of lamb. Occasionally, the menu was varied with a delicious piece of salted fish, or the occasional egg that the hens laid at this time of year. Often, she found some dried vegetables on her doorstep. The children were especially delighted when some dried fruit came their way. There was always dried corn that she could grind with her mortar and pestle to make cornbread or cornmeal. The bread that she made each day was very much the food staple.

When she was not cooking or tending to her brood, Lydia turned to cleaning her house, which largely involved the endless task of sweeping the earthen floor which had been packed hard, but still there were always bits of dirt here and there that the children had kicked up when playing. Lydia always had an eye out for any signs of vermin that were inclined to seek shelter from the cold, and always seemed to be able to find a crack through which to escape it. She also kept a keen eye out for signs of fleas and bedbugs that were a constant nuisance. Although her possessions were meager, she was grateful that George had found time to build two crude cots for his children who slept in the loft above, a tiny cot for

Sally who slept beside her parents, and the rough-hewn bedstead for them. Fortunately, the trestle table and benches in front of the fireplace that had greeted them when they first arrived had been made for them to keep. For now, this was sufficient until George could find time to build a few cupboards and chests to hold the contents of the wagon that now lay in a corner, because the wagon needed to be used for other purposes. Laundry day was especially burdensome in the winter, and with her growing family it seemed to come around with alarming speed.

As spring finally came, the hours of daylight lengthened, and the snow and ice that had encased the countryside throughout the winter slowly began to disappear. George was finally able to turn his attention to further enhancements of his barnyard and fencing. By using the wood that he had harvested the previous fall, he was able to strengthen and expand the structure for his animals that had been built before he first arrived. He lengthened the makeshift fenced enclosure that had carried them through the winter so his animals had a larger area in which to stay. It seemed like it took forever for the land to dry out from the winter thaw but, at last, by mid-May, George could begin to work his small parcel of land. He was grateful that during the winter Levi would sometimes let him use the Anchor Shop forge to construct the plow and sledge that would be invaluable tools in the months ahead.

After he finished work at the Anchor Shop, George could get in a few hours of work. With a bit of still warm sunshine on his back, and his hat pulled down firmly over his brow, he set forth each late afternoon to hitch up his team and work his bit of land. He was grateful that he had been able to clear some of the forest land that lay behind his house before winter hit. After a long period with little to do his oxen had become restive. They too were eager to get to the land. When they saw their master appear, they shook their huge heads, and then remembered to lower them to receive the yoke that George placed upon their massive shoulders. A treat always came after they were securely yoked.

As his team pulled the plow, George gripped the two wood bars that attached to the sturdy iron vee apparatus that he had fabricated at the Anchor Shop. While guiding his team and the plow before him, he watched carefully for roots and rocks that could cause great damage if not avoided. He mentally noted where they were, although they were usually easy enough to see, and planned to come back later with his sledge and a long, iron pry bar that he would use to roll them onto it. As he worked in the open, he found it immensely satisfying to feel the soft earth gently turning to either side as the plow dug in, and he deeply inhaled in order to savor its pungent spring-like odor. It seemed that the earth was coming to life before him. Now at last, he would be able to grow the crops that he would need to feed his animals during the winter months.

George was mindful that Lydia needed a garden in which to grow her vegetables, berries, and herbs. This demanded a more refined type of soil preparation than for the pasture or land upon which to grow crops for the animals. First, he plowed the earth and removed any rocks or roots, just as he had done in the other areas. Then, he began to laboriously turn the land by hand in order to create the fine soil that her garden required. He carefully broke each clod of earth into smaller and smaller pieces. Then, he took some of the manure created by his animals over the winter, spread it out evenly and worked it in carefully. It was a lengthy, but satisfying, process, and as he did so he could not help thinking of all the wonderful things that would be on their table in the coming growing season. He was eager for it to get a bit warmer so that he could plant the seeds that Lydia had brought with her from home. In the meantime, he built a netting enclosure around her garden that he prayed would keep animals such as rabbits and deer from nibbling the tiny, succulent plants as they burst forth from the soil. Later on, he thought that he might be able to build a sturdy wall with all of the rocks that he had pulled out of the soil.

HAPPY YEARS FOR GEORGE
AND LYDIA

By early summer, with all of this accomplished, and the hours of daylight increasing steadily, he was able to turn his attention toward increasing his livestock. Onc of his first acquisitions was a cow. This gentle beast provided his family with the milk the children needed to grow strong bones, and she always seemed so relieved when he came to lighten her load each morning and evening after he milked her. George then took the warm, frothy buckets of milk into the house where Lydia would let it settle, then skim off the cream that had risen to the surface and set it aside to churn into butter when she had the time.

He bought several fine young sows from a farmer who lived just outside of the village, and he drove them home squeaking and snorting all the way. He knew that they would grub out almost anything, whether it was the roots that were still in the ground after the trees were felled or keeping thistles and nettles from cropping up in his newly created field. He figured that he could use a neighbor's boar from time to time to further increase his passel of swine and have more pork for his family. In time, he added a small flock of ewes and a ram to his livestock, with the hope that the flock would grow over time. Lamb was a favored meat for him and Lydia, and the sheep's wool was a very precious commodity, as the harsh winters in this northern clime demanded warm clothing if one was to withstand the bitter cold and biting wind. Layers of woven or knitted woolen garments presented the best possible solution and Lydia was agile with spinning, carding and knitting. She was grateful that she had brought her small spinning wheel with her on the journey. She also knew just how to sew a woolen garment, and then shrink it in a large vat of boiling water so that the weave would tighten, and the garment would better protect its wearer from the freezing elements.

His flock of domestic fowl grew as George acquired some ducks, geese, and turkeys. Although the cranky hens had taken this addition adversely in the beginning, they were all getting along now. Orrin who was four, and George who was three, loved being asked to do special things that made them feel grown up. They were particularly skillful at fetch and carry tasks, so every morning, with baskets in hand, they ran out to the barnyard to gather the eggs that the hens had so graciously laid for them. Then, they put their plump little hands into the sack full of chicken feed and scattered it for the waiting fowl. They were always amused that the hens remained patiently waiting until the rooster had ingested his share first.

George's neighbors who had come to Willsborough before him had quickly discovered that there was always a plentitude of fish in both the Boquet River and out in Lake Champlain. When they could, he and other community members went down to the mouth of the river where they put in the huge seines that they had woven together during the winter in order to catch large quantities of fish. Although using these seines in the river and the lake provided them with a variety of fish, including northern and walleye pike, perch, and bass, the seines were especially useful when capturing the vast quantities of salmon that lived in the lake and swam upstream to spawn in the Spring.[54] Their catches were often extensive, and when salted or smoked these fish provided the fishermen's families with delicious variety.

Upon occasion, George was able to walk along the riverbank, and on down to the lake with young George and Orrin, and their friends. Polly had to stay at home to help her mother with Sally who was wont to get into lots of mischief and, anyway, she had been told that fishing was not for girls. Each of the boys carried crude fishing poles that their fathers had helped them to make, and a basket just in case they caught something. As they walked, they would pause briefly from time to time to cast their lines into the water where it eddied into a pool behind a large rock. Sometimes, a fish really would bite, and then there was great excitement as George helped them to reel in their catch and put it into their basket. If it was a very warm day, the children would beg to go into the water where it was particularly shallow and calm. Orrin and George would roll up their pants legs to their knees and wade out just far enough so that they could splash one another, laughing gleefully as they did so, until George called them back to the riverbank.

Lydia too, eagerly embraced the lengthening days and the increasing warmth of the sun as the long winter ebbed. The transition from darkness and cold to light and warmth came more slowly than she wished, but she had learned to be patient. By mid-May, on bright and sunny days, she no longer had to tend the fire night and day. If she banked it well, it would quickly come back to life for the cooking of each meal. Now, she could throw open the door and the few small windows of their house to let fresh air and light stream in. She breathed deeply and went about her chores with fresh energy as she swept away the cobwebs that had not been visible in winter's darkness and cleaned her home from top to bottom.

Even laundry day seemed less daunting to Lydia. During the cold months, this had been an especially arduous undertaking. She filled her big cast-iron pots with the water that George had left in leather buckets inside the door and set these on the bed of hot coals in the fireplace that she had created. While the water was heating, she gathered all of the soiled articles and sorted them into piles because she always washed the least dirty items first when the water was nice and clean. When the water was just beginning to bubble, she very carefully removed the heavy pots from the fire and poured their contents into two tin wash tubs, one for washing and one for rinsing. Then, she tackled the often-exhausting job of scrubbing the clothes on her rough scrub board with the lye soap that she had brought from home. As she lifted the dripping wet clothes from the rinse tub, she wrapped them around her broomstick to wring them out before she hung them up to dry on the ropes George had hung between the rafters.

When George came home from his day's work at the Anchor Shop, he would empty the tin tubs. Occasionally, she would repeat the process of preparing the water for washing, only this time it was for the family bath ritual. It began with little Sally, then the children and herself and, finally, George who was always the dirtiest. The children loved this occasion and delighted in singing and splashing one another until Lydia called a halt to the activity. Now that summer had come, it was so much easier. She could drape the clothes over the fence or a bush and everyone could bathe outdoors.

Best of all, Lydia treasured the moments when she and her friends could gather together. She felt blessed that even though she had been in Willsborough for such a short time, and much of it had been spent in the isolation of winter, she had made some very dear friends and was feeling increasingly less homesick for friends and family back in Canaan. She had grown particularly close to Levi Higby's wife, Chloe, and to George Throop's wife who was a relative of Chloe's. After their chores were complete, the women would gather at one another's homes, or along the banks of the river if the weather was fine. They usually brought a bit of sewing or knitting with them and kept their hands busy as they were chatting. With their little ones beside them, they would exchange news, talk about their daily lives, console those who had lost a loved one, and express their love for one another.

With the warmer weather, the children rejoiced in running out to play without the hindrance of many layers of clothing and heavy boots to slow them down. Shouts and laughter accompanied them on their adventures as they played tag, rolled hoops and tossed balls between one another. In addition to fishing, their father would take the boys down by the river where they watched for salmon to come swimming upstream with their tails flicking as they leaped over obstacles and sought a place to spawn in the gravelly bottom where the water ran over rapids.[55] Life was good!

Every day during those lovely warm months, Lydia would go out to the fine garden that George had planted for her. She found it most pleasant to tend her plantings in the early morning hours, before the sun got too strong. She enjoyed the solitude and time to herself before her busy day began, and often crept out to her garden before anyone in the family had arisen. With the long winter that she knew would come inevitably once again, she wanted to be sure that she had vegetables that she could store in the small root cellar that George had dug out under the cabin. There, she put her parsnips, potatoes, rutabaga, turnips, winter squash, onions, garlic, carrots, and beets. She put them in sacks and hung them from the beams above her head to prevent vermin from getting into them, and then she hung some aromatics from her herb garden to make her produce even less attractive. During the summer months, her family really enjoyed treats such as peas and green beans, cabbage, leeks and cucumbers and some of the summer squash that seemed to thrive in her climate. Summer was also a time for pickling, and Lydia had found that beets, cabbage, horseradish, peppers, radishes, and onions were delicious when preserved this way. She would soak them in brine to draw out the moisture, and then place the dried vegetables in a barrel or pot of vinegar to complete the process. Occasionally, she would pickle eggs, as well as a few types of fish, although she generally preferred to salt or smoke the latter. [56]

Lydia was especially proud of her fine herb garden, and she particularly liked basil, dill, oregano, parsley, sage, rosemary and thyme, all of which she used frequently to enhance the flavor of the dishes that she prepared. More importantly, many of the herbs that she grew had strong medicinal value. She had found that mint and thyme really helped her family with a wide variety of stomach complaints, and she always had lemon balm and lamb's ear on hand to dress the wounds that her children frequently had after a fun-filled day of play. Yarrow really helped to stanch the blood if their injuries were more serious. She loved rosemary and lavender because they made her house smell sweet and kept vermin away. Biting insects were always a problem and rue and tansy often helped to repel them.[57]

All of Lydia's family loved both the wild and cultivated berries that were plentiful in the summer, and George had built her a small grape arbor. She preferred to keep the best of these fruits for their daily use and used the less perfect ones to make jams and jellies.[58] Days when she was making these were very special for the children who were always rewarded with a taste. During that first summer, George had planted the beginnings of a small orchard that would begin to bear fruit in a few years. Chloe had told her that apples, cherries, plums and pears did well in their area, and Lydia had learned to dry these fruits back in Canaan where she had spent early evenings preparing them to be strung before the fireplace in order to dry properly for later use. Once these foodstuffs were dried sufficiently she would carry them up the ladder to store them in the loft where the older children slept. She was delighted that one day she would have fruit trees of her own.

As a long summer day came to an end, Lydia attended to her final chores while George took care of the needs of his livestock. She cleaned up the dishes, cutlery and cooking vessels after their light evening meal and let the fire go out. It was such a pleasure not to have to bank it carefully so that there would be embers in the morning, as she had to do in the winter. Then, she readied the children for bed, and helped them up the ladder to the loft. That done, she finally was able to attend to her spinning, weaving, sewing, mending and knitting. For now, she reveled in having a bit of natural light still pouring through the cabin door. As she sat working quietly, she loved hearing the contented sounds of the animals, and smelling the pleasant barnyard aroma as it wafted through the air toward her.

Summer days with their warmth and sunshine seemed to fly by, and before he knew it, George noticed that the days were getting shorter and night was descending upon them earlier. Geese began wheeling through the air in huge vees, honking loudly and landing in any field where there was a morsel of grain or corn for them to feast upon before their journey south. The gulls swung over the lake more slowly as they too prepared to fly south toward warmer places. Leaves were turning and dropping from the trees and shades of yellow and brilliant red lay on the ground. The air began to take on the aroma of fall as fireplaces burned more frequently. Change was in the air once again.

Like most people in his community as George faced his second winter, he had found various means of augmenting his family's food supply during those fall months. He had been very successful bringing down geese from the flocks as they flew overhead, as well as shooting the ducks that inhabited the shores of the river near the village. He had also discovered that grouse were plentiful and quite delicious to eat. He had begun to set forth with rifle in hand, often just after dawn, in search of the deer, squirrels, raccoons, and even bears, that inhabited the forests around the village. These too would provide sustenance for himself and his family and, in the case of shooting the bears, it would give his family and livestock greater security. Although many of his fellow citizens set traps for these animals, he had decided that, unless he was desperate for meat, he would make the demise of his prey more painless by shooting them.

Early November was the time for butchering the larger animals, and butchering days were very busy for everyone. This was a community affair, and men from near and far helped one another with the task. The men's job was to slaughter the animal, split it open, and then hang it from a sturdy hook so that all of the blood and entrails would flow out onto the ground. Once this had been accomplished, they would carefully skin the animal, retaining the hide to tan and turn into leather at a later date. Their final task was to cut the meat into large chunks.[59] After this, they handed the process to the women who, like the men, had come together to help one another.

Although far along in her pregnancy, Lydia worked with the other women as well as she could. As they chatted among themselves, they went about the business of cutting up the meat that the men had prepared and turning it into more usable pieces. They liked to salt their beef and lamb in order to draw the moisture out of it and preserve it for as long as possible, so they rubbed the freshly cut pieces of meat with a thick mixture of salt and saltpeter, or niter, which was used to keep the meat pinkish and looking fresh. Once the moisture had been removed, they repeated the salting process over and over to form a thick crust that would protect the meat from insects and mold. When this was accomplished, they put the salted meat in a cool place, or sometimes they packed it in straw in a barrel.[60]

The women preferred to smoke the pork, so they cut the carcasses into large pieces, surrounded them with salt and put them into tubs that had holes in the bottom to let any further moisture out.[61] Then, it was ready to be smoked. George did not have a smokehouse, but fortunately one of his neighbors had one that he was willing to share with others. When the neighbor had built a fire in the center of the windowless and flueless building, all was in readiness. George hauled his pork over to the smokehouse where his neighbor hung it from hooks in the ceiling and then left it there for several weeks until it was thoroughly dried out and had a thick coating of soot around it from the smoke.[62] He then rubbed it with a bit of pepper to keep the insects away. For those like Lydia and George who had no space to hang the meat before using it, the neighbor was willing to keep it hung away from rodents and other vermin in return for being given a portion of the meat.

On November 28, 1802, Lydia gave birth to her fifth child, Lucy Mira. She, like most women, had not been able to lighten her load of tasks and responsibilities during her pregnancy, and she had found standing for long periods during the butchering season had been very taxing. Several of her friends helped her through a long and painful delivery, and because of her weakened condition, they shared the responsibility for helping her as much as they could during her time of need, which they referred to as "sickness". Taking care of Lydia, her four children, and now her new baby, was not a simple task for these women who had families of their own to tend to. Once again, Lydia and George experienced the love and care of their new community. Willsborough was truly home!

GOOD YEARS FOR ALL

As the years rolled on, in a pattern that often seemed to repeat itself, George's family continued to increase. On May 14, 1804, two-year-old Lucy Mira and her four other siblings were joined by a brother, Calvin Bethewel. With eight family members, thirty-two-year-old Lydia's life was largely consumed by meeting the various needs of her family, including seeing that they were fed, clothed, and kept alive just as she had in the years before. It just got a bit harder with the addition of each child. Like so many of her friends, she had little time to think about anything else. Summer gave her a bit of a respite. She loved those warm sunny days when she could gather with others her own age, and they had the opportunity to share experiences and concerns while they watched their children play around them. She felt like she was coming alive once again. The winters were very hard times for her, as they were for everyone. Those were the seemingly endless days when she felt isolated and alone.

Sometimes, Lydia envied George because he got away from the cabin each day. However, she was grateful that he liked his work at the Anchor Shop and had been very successful there. His proficiency and willingness to work hard had earned him a position of great trust and respect among his coworkers. Levi and George had come to rely upon him increasingly, and they felt very comfortable leaving him in charge if they had business elsewhere. George felt very fulfilled by his life and grateful that he was able to provide for his wife and growing brood. He enjoyed working his small parcel of land and truly appreciated time with his animals. He had grown to love Willsborough and felt so comfortable there. Much to his surprise, he did not miss farming at all.

In 1804, Levi had taken on responsibility as both the town's postmaster and supervisor, in addition to his oversight of the Anchor Shop, so he highly valued the help that he got from George. In this same year, there were nine taverns and inns in the town, and prominent community members, including Abraham Aiken, Belden Noble, James Reynolds, Thomas Stafford, and even Levi, were owners of these.[63] George was amazed that Levi was able to handle so many responsibilities when, between his own work, his family, his home, his small parcel of land, and his animals he found that he had little time to take on any other obligations.

As the town continued to grow, it faced a rapidly increasing threat from wolves that seemed to proliferate as the land became more open. Whole packs of them were coming down from the mountains each night in search of both farm and town livestock upon which they could feed. In response to this devastating situation, a town ordinance was established whereby any person killing a wolf would receive a bounty of $3.00.[64] George had experienced the viciousness of the wolves one night when they got into his enclosure. Fortunately, he heard the ruckus almost immediately, ran out with the rifle that always lay beside his bed, and shot three of them before they had done too much harm. He was happy that the town recognized the seriousness of this situation, and glad to receive his $9.00 bounty for the wolves whose lives he had ended.

On his excursions along the river, George had always been amazed by the amount of wood that came rushing down from the south, and through the town. He liked to follow the wood-laden river as it went under the bridge, past the wing dam where the Anchor Shop was, around the sharp bend in the river, and then on its final leg to Lake Champlain. When he walked to the mouth of the river, he watched an awaiting crew of men lash the timbers together to form a raft that they could power by a sail or paddles, depending upon the winds and weather conditions, as they piloted the raft on its way north to Canada.

One day, he asked Levi why all of this wood was going to Canada, and Levi explained that it was all due to something called the Jay Treaty that had been made between England and the United States in 1795. England's great forests had been depleted so badly that this once heavily forested country had had to look elsewhere for wood for fuel and construction. The Champlain Valley was an ideal source since it had accessible waterways that connected directly to the ocean via the Richelieu and St. Lawrence Rivers. This made transport much easier. Also, there was an abundance of virgin timber and settlers needed to fell trees in order to clear the land for farms and settlements. Pine was especially abundant in the area and loggers were eager to send it on its way across the Atlantic. As a very light wood, it was easy to float down the river to Lake Champlain in large quantities. The British Navy especially prized oak for ship masts because of its strength and resiliency and there was also plenty of that all along Lake Champlain.[65]

George was fascinated that the wood that was being rafted north was actually on its way across the ocean to England. The thought of anything going that far was somewhat overwhelming to one whose world suddenly seemed very small, even though he knew that the anchors that he helped to make went a long distance on their various ships. He had also noticed that the amount of timber that was floated down the river increased each year as the profits reaped from sending it through Canada, and on to England, soared. Farmers and speculators alike were gaining huge benefits from this trade.

By 1805, the town was forced to establish new regulations to bring some control over this huge wood trade, especially where riverbanks and property were in danger. A new ordinance stated that anyone who had timbers more than fourteen feet long had to cut them into shorter lengths and would have to pay a fee of $5 for every 24 hours that the longer lengths remained in the river. Tree trunks that could be cut up for timber, including those used for building materials and rafts were called sawlogs and were exempt from the ordinance.[66]

This ordinance was specifically aimed at preventing logjams that did huge devastation when they occurred, and it was very strictly enforced especially during the spring flooding season. As a law-abiding citizen, George felt that he should help when there was a logjam. He was strong, a good planner and manager, and well respected by the men who worked with him as a team. He enjoyed the challenges of this work even though it was inherently dangerous. There was always concern for the wood bridge, which served as a lifeline to the outside world to the north and west. Losing it would be catastrophic. George understood the necessity of the ordinance and supported it wholeheartedly. Fortunately, he was not sending logs to the north, so it did not directly impact him as it did some others. He had heard certain community members complain mightily about the ordinance and actively defy it.

George Throop, who was as enterprising as his business partner Levi, established an ashery on the hillside above the bridge in response to the booming potash trade with England that had developed.[67] England was faced with yet another critical shortage as a result of its lack of wood. It could not make the potash that was a critical ingredient for manufacturing glass, dye for textiles, and lye for soap. It was also used to scour the freshly shorn fleeces from England's huge sheep population and to clean flax.[68] As a result, it was very profitable to supply potash to England just as it was to send wood across the Atlantic.

As community members were felling trees in order to create more open land for pasture and crop, they were happy to bring their hardwoods to the ashery. George found the process for making potash quite fascinating. He watched as the wood was burned until it became nothing more than very fine ash, and then one of the workers would leach it with water to create lye. After that, he saw a worker take the lye mixture and pour it into big iron pots and put them over the open fire so that eventually they would boil down so completely that there was only a thick, ashy deposit left.[69] This was put in barrels and shipped to England or kept for use at home.

The year 1805 brought other major changes to the area. Essex County was formed in 1799, and the 1792 blockhouse in Willsborough that had never been used to fend off an Indian uprising, became the courthouse and jail. George, like many others, was shocked when on April 2, 1805, portions of Willsborough were split off to form Lewis and Essex and make them separate entities,[70] just as Willsborough had been formed from Crown Point in 1788. This meant that the blockhouse was no longer part of Willsborough and, suddenly, Essex was the county seat and not Willsborough. Fortunately, the jealousy that erupted was short-lived and Elizabethtown, or "Pleasant Valley", as it was commonly referred to, became the geographically more central county seat in 1807.[71] George was glad that he was too busy to pay much attention to these political goings-on or get involved in some of the hard feelings that were precipitated by these changes.

By 1805, Willsborough had also experienced a proliferation of taverns and inns, and the total had risen to eighteen.[72] Because of this excess, the Town had actually formed a Committee of Excise whose responsibility was to ensure that the owners of these businesses paid the taxes they owed.[73] Four years earlier, Levi had also built a brewery and distillery just up the hill to serve the taverns.[74] Of course, he kept the very best for his own tavern and George, very wisely, was loyal to Levi's tavern, although he did go to others from time to time. Especially on long winter evenings, after his chores were done and his children were in bed, he would go to a tavern when it was dark and there was nothing else to do. While Lydia, like many wives in that day, did not approve of the drinking that was taking place, she knew how much this meant to her husband. So, with a kiss on the cheek he would set out with lantern in hand and head down the hill to where he and his friends came together to hear the news, exchange bits of gossip and intrigue, or play darts. In this still newly formed nation, the national political scene was of particular interest even in this far-flung region so, while indulging in a pint of ale or perhaps some rum, the conversations could become quite boisterous. Occasionally, a brawl would have to be broken up. As the rum flowed eloquence did so equally!

The inns were a favorite place for travelers who needed to stop for a night before reaching their final destination which might lie to the north or south, or even across the lake. Travel up and down the lake always involved an element of peril. Wild animals lurked in the forests, robbers frequented the well-used routes, and there were tales that Indians might be lurking in the mountains ready to pounce upon the unsuspecting traveler. George was well aware of this since he had been told of these things when he was planning his route north and west from Canaan. Travelers were glad to spend a night without fear no matter how mean the accommodations were.

The inns were also frequented by peddlers who were passing through on a time-honored route and timetable to trade goods, usually several times a year. Lydia looked forward to their visits. She was able to procure things that she could not make herself, or were not available in the village and, as importantly, she got news from places beyond her narrow horizon. Both peddlers and travelers played a vital role in life in Willsborough because they brought all sorts of news about what was going on in the rest of the Champlain Valley and beyond.

George, like many members of his community, was keenly aware that his own education was minimal. He barely had the most basic reading, writing and addition skills. He and many other townspeople wanted their children to have a better opportunity for book learning than they had had, and so they were eager to have a proper school for them. In 1806, when John Morhous moved the location of his store to a plot further uphill, the town took over his former building in order to create a schoolhouse.[75] During the winter, when the older boys were not needed to help as much with outside chores, and the girls with helping with cooking and childcare, they were free to attend school. Younger children, and girls were more likely to be regular attendees at the new school. Because Lydia desperately needed Polly's help with the children she, like many eldest daughters in large families, seldom was able to attend. However, Orrin and George went down the hill to school each day and both of them seemed eager to learn. This gave their parents great pleasure.

On April 8, 1806, George and Lydia's seventh child, Lydia Amanda, arrived. With each addition to her family, Lydia's life became even more stressful. With each childbirth, she could feel more and more of her strength begin to be taken from her. While she thanked God that she had not suffered the loss of a child, she prayed that He would not send her any more offspring. With seven children, plus themselves, their tiny house was bursting at the seams, and Lydia did not think that she could handle anything more.

As the year 1807 rolled in, Willsborough continued to grow and flourish. Those who lived outside of the village began to refer to it as "The Falls", instead of Willsborough because of presence of the significant falls there, and those in the village quickly moved toward that "nickname". By this time, the number of farmers outside of the village and squatters out on Willsborough Point had continued to increase significantly enough that there were two highway districts even out there.[76]

As the town kept growing, its population of animals, as well as people, increased. So, in 1807, there were enough irresponsible livestock owners that a new ordinance had to be put in place. From then on, horses, hogs, and sheep that were not viewed as free commoners were not allowed to range freely within the town. For some reason, cows were not included because they were considered to cause less overall devastation.[77] Free Commoners were those who were entitled to have their livestock in the common area that had been set aside. George was grateful that he was among those who were deemed to be Free Commoners. His piece of land was adequate for his purposes, except that it did not allow a place where he could take his animals to graze freely in a space that was larger than his plot of land would allow. He was horrified that people who owned non-castrated male animals would countenance letting them loose to run freely during mating season and fully supported the ordinance that stated quite clearly that these animals could be caught by the Pound Master, who then had the right to sell them.

March 13, 1807 marked a significant achievement in Essex County. In a period when turnpikes proliferated, the Essex County Turnpike Company was the first turnpike stock company to be formed there. Its founders included many of the men who were highly recognized in the area. Among them were: Jonathan Lynde, Thomas Stower, Abraham Aiken, Belden Noble, Joseph Sheldon, Stephen Cuyler and, of course Levi Higby and George Throop. The company was authorized to build a turnpike from Grog Harbor north to where it intersected the Great Northern Turnpike. A thousand shares were sold at $25 per share.[78] This road connected the northern part of Lake George and Elizabethtown, the new Essex County seat, via Port Henry.[79] This was a tremendous boon to the area and opened up many new trade routes and opportunities for economic development and further settlement.

At this time, it was recognized that there were a growing number of boundary line disputes since surveyors could not keep up with the huge demands for their time and skills, especially out on the Point where the number of settlers was rapidly increasing. Some of these disputes involved relatively small tracts of land and were seen as a mere nuisance. However, in 1807, several of these disputes became of such consequence that Thomas Stower was appointed specifically to ascertain the north line between Willsborough and Chesterfield, as well as the south boundary between Brookfield and Willsborough.[80] George was greatly relieved that he lived in the village with a small plot of land, and was surrounded by neighbors who were content with their holdings.

THE COMMUNITY'S EMBRACE
IN TRAGEDY

Sometime in the spring of 1807, George Throop and Levi Higby sent George to West Troy, where the Navy distribution center was located. Because they had come to view him as a completely trustworthy individual, they often chose him for important missions, such as this one, especially those that involved money. As usual, after bidding farewell to his family, George set out on horseback, this time bearing $1500 worth of Federal specie (gold and silver coins) in his leather saddlebag.[81] Tragically, after those six very happy early years in Willsborough, this trip, that seemed quite routine, would change the lives of George and his family forever.

Throop and Higby had anticipated that George would return within a few weeks at the very outside. However, those weeks rolled by as day after day anxiously passed by, and he did not return or send any news of his whereabouts. Needless to say, his employers became very concerned, and Lydia was filled with worry and fear that something terrible had happened to him. As time went on, people began to conjure up all sorts of ideas as to what might have occurred. Some thought that, having lost all scruples, he simply took off with the money. This seemed too atypical of George's behavior for anyone to really believe. Others were concerned that he was waylaid by thieves who killed him and took the money. If that were the case, the unanswered question was what they would have done with his body since it had not yet been found. Some even conjectured that a band of marauding Indians had attacked and killed him, although this seemed unlikely since there were few reports of marauding Indians on the route he traversed. No one would ever know the real story. He was simply never heard from again, and by the June 5, 1807 meeting of the Town of Willsborough Board his name was erased from the list of citizens.

With the tragic disappearance, and probable death of her husband, Lydia and her children were catapulted into a state of vast upheaval. Like so many widows in that day, thirty-five-year-old Lydia suddenly found herself penniless and with no means of caring for herself or her seven children, the youngest of whom was only a year old and the eldest just twelve. She thought of trying to connect with her father and mother who she believed still lived in Stillwater, New York. As we know, she had lost communication with them after she had left her parents and moved back to her birthplace in Canaan, Litchfield, Connecticut as a young girl.

After Lydia and George were married, George had tried to break the silence between his wife and her family, and to restore the family relationship. On October 20, 1796, he wrote to her parents, Phineas and Hannah Jakeways, saying:

Dear Father and Mother,

I take this opportunity to right to you and yours to inform you that we are all well at present and I hope that these few lines will find you so. We were married April 23, 1794 and we had a daughter born February the 28, 1795 and her name is called Polle and all had the measles beginning on August last and we was very sick about four weeks. I hope God will permit us to meet in love again for I have not forgotten some of the family. My greatest love to every one of you. Mr. Freeman tells us all is well with you.

Please give Hannah and the rest our best.

George Clark.

Once again there was no response from either of Lydia's parents.

Now, twelve years later, and following the loss of her husband in early 1807, Lydia tried to reach out to her father once again. She wrote and begged him for support in her time of need. In this very poignant letter she explained her desperate plight and asked him to provide shelter for herself and her children. She said:

Honored Father,

I wish to know what is the matter. Do you disown your children when motherless? Not one word from a father... I have had everything ready to come and see you all. I am father and mother too... This with all the blessing of God from your ever- faithful child.

Lydia Clark, Willsborough.

In that same letter, she begged to know if her Uncle Calvin knew anything about George's whereabouts. Unfortunately, her pleas to her father were to no avail, and her uncle was not able to share any news about George's whereabouts.

It is hard to imagine how difficult life must have been for this young widow who had so many children to tend to and feed. Being of stalwart stock, she faced the challenges with determination and energy. Fortunately, Willsborough had established a Poor Fund that was overseen by a group of elected town officials. Its sole purpose was to assist those who found themselves in dire financial straits due to a host of different circumstances. It had never occurred to Lydia that she would be one of the Fund's recipients, but she accepted the assistance with a grateful heart. Not one to receive charity easily, she was also determined to find every possible way in which to help herself.

In the true spirit of a caring community, Lydia's friends and neighbors reached out to her in countless different ways. If they had more to eat than they needed they would offer some of their bounty to Lydia and her children. This was particularly important when it came to meat. With so much responsibility and the challenges that she faced each day Lydia had given up the livestock that George had accumulated. During butchering time, friends would put aside a small portion for the Clarks, and Lydia would often join the other women as they cut, salted or prepared the meat for smoking, drying, or storage. When sheep were being shorn, a portion of wool always appeared on Lydia's doorstep, and in the fall, when the cold winds of winter were not far behind, neighbors would bring wood to her and neatly stack it outside her door.

Mercifully, prior to his disappearance, George had prepared the garden for Lydia that had been well-tilled and was rich with humus. She knew that the seeds that she planted would grow quickly and ripen into produce that would provide her family with plenty of fresh food during the summer months. As the days became longer, and the sun a bit warmer, she was able to begin sowing the seeds that she had gathered from the previous year's crops. Orrin, age nine, George age eight, and Sally, age seven, were eager to help their mother and cheerfully went about assisting with the easier portion of the work. Meanwhile, Lydia, who relied upon twelve-year-old Polly in countless ways, left the three youngest children in her care so that she could tend to her garden.

During the summer, she tended her plot of vegetables with loving care. The little family enjoyed their summer repasts of fresh vegetables. When her land seemed a bit parched, she brought water from the well and poured it over the thirsty plants, and when weeds began to appear in the neat rows that she had created Orrin, George, and Sally went about the task of clearing these with nimble fingers. Even the littlest children delighted in being outdoors and near the garden. They loved to run the fertile soil through their fingers and watch it tumble down to the earth as the wind caught it. Frequently, they were admonished when they could not resist reaching out to pluck leaves, or even an entire plant from the earth.

The small orchard that George had put in was now fully mature. Apples, plums, and pears bowed down their branches with the weight of the fruits that they bore. The grape arbor was covered with succulent fruit that fairly beckoned to be picked and the blueberry, blackberry, and raspberry bushes were laden with sweet morsels to be eaten. Lydia had covered the berries with a rough net, but the birds would swoop down and seemed to always find a small entry point. The children, of course, rejoiced in the opportunity to simply pluck the fruit and pop it into their mouths, with the juice fairly running down their little chins. Oh such joy!

Harvest was a very special time in the lives of those who lived off what they could draw from their land and the whole family was able to participate in some way. With Polly's help and oversight, the littlest ones could carry small baskets laden with fruit to their waiting mother. The older children were responsible for actually picking the fruits that were within their reach and could even climb the ladders to access the grapes on the arbor and the fruits on the trees. Meanwhile, Lydia packed the fruits that could be preserved for a bit longer in straw and placed them in the cool, dark cellar. She and Polly boiled the fruits that could not be preserved as they were picked and created jams that would provide the sweetness that enhanced every meal all year around. Lydia and Polly spent evenings slicing the apples, pears and plums and then stringing them and hanging them in the attic to dry for future use.

Lydia was also very proud of her fowl. She took good care of them and let her children help with their endeavor in any way that they could. Her roosters did a fine job of keeping the hens under control, and proudly strutted back and forth each morning as they saluted the sunrise with a very loud cockle doodle-do. The hens meanwhile actively engaged in plucking every possible grub or worm from the soil during the day, and then retired to rest and lay their eggs as night came upon them. Lydia's youngest children delighted in going out to the coop in the morning, reaching into each nesting box, and then proudly displaying the day's gift before gently laying the egg into the awaiting basket. The ducks were a source of joy as well as nourishment. It was uncanny that they always knew where home was. When they were released from their cage each morning and had partaken of the morning's repast of corn and grain that the children brought to them they would waddle their way down to the river and swim delightedly up and down. Yet, when the first sign of the sun's shadow lengthened they would make their way back up to their home. If startled by a passing animal, they were even known to take flight. The gaggle of geese were another story. They always seemed to be a bit angry at the world and would flap their wings aggressively if something that they perceived to be an enemy came near them. Needless to say, the children quickly learned to give them a wide berth. Lydia always made sure that all of these creatures were enclosed before nightfall lest a wandering wolf or other animal of prey viewed them as a tasty treat.

Lydia found still other ways to keep her family together and happy. She loved her friends and neighbors and seized every opportunity to assist those in need and reciprocate their many kindnesses to her. When she heard of anyone in any kind of distress, she would leave Polly in charge as always. Lydia had become skillful as a midwife and was often called at any hour of the day or night to assist with a birth, especially one that was not going well. She frequently stayed on a bit longer just to be sure that both mother and child were doing well. She tended the sick and invalids with tenderness and compassion, and often put into use the medicinal herbs that she had grown in her garden and then dried. When death was lurking at the door, she joined those who watched until the person's last breath had been taken. Then, she would join the women who laid out the body in preparation for its final resting place. Neighbors and friends often referred to Lydia as "Nurse Lydia" because of the many ways in which she came to the aid of others. Needless to say, those whom she had helped were eager to reach out to her in any way that they could.

Each day was like a miracle for Lydia and she often wondered what she would have done if her life had taken a similar tragic course in another place. The residents of Willsborough and its surrounding communities had been so good to her. She always began her day thanking God for the many blessings that He had bestowed upon her and praying that she would be able to do for others in the future just as was being done for her.

In 1810, Lydia finally received a long-awaited answer to her prayers. Her father, Phineas,[82] after shirking his daughter for three years, pleaded with his daughter to come to live with him in Stillwater, New York and to bring her young offspring with her. This sudden change of heart appears to have been precipitated by the death of his wife, Hannah, and Phineas' need to have a woman in his house.[83]

Lydia and her little family packed up their goods, just as they had done when they had departed from Canaan nine years earlier. They shared tears and warm embraces with the friends and neighbors who had been so good to them and said their farewell to a community that had been such a wonderful home. Then, turning to the south, they embarked upon the journey that would take them to their new home in Stillwater, Saratoga County, New York.

Lydia and her children, with the exception of Orrin who had been indentured prior to their departure for Stillwater, no longer play a role in our story. Instead, in the book to come, our journey with the Clark family will continue with Lydia's firstborn son, Orrin, who played a prominent role in Willsborough throughout his long life.

REFERENCES

Baldwin, Betsy. *The Antiquarian*, Clinton County Historical Association, Plattsburgh, NY. Issue 37. 1992.

Downes, Alice Higby. *The Story of an Old Home in Willsboro, New York*, Unpublished. 1927.

Glenn, Morris F. *Story of Three Towns*. Morris Glenn. 1977.

McGrory Klyza, Christopher and Trombulak, Stephen C. *The Story of Vermont: A Natural and Cultural History*. University Press of New England. 2015.

Muller, H. Nicholas III. Jay's Treaty: The Transformation of Lake Champlain Commerce. Vermont History, *The proceedings of the Vermont Historical Society*, Winter/Spring 2012.

Nading Hill, Ralph. *Two Centuries of Ferry Boating*. Lake Champlain Transportation Company. 1972.

Olmert, Michael. Smokehouse, Foursquare and Solid, Colonial. *Williamsburg Journal*, Winter 2004-2005.

Sherman, Gordon, C., Sherman, Elsie L. *Ferries of the Champlain Valley and Adirondack Mountains. 929 years of History.* Vol. II 1814-1929. Elisabethtown, NY: Denton Publications. 2007.

Smith, H.P. *History of Essex County*. Syracuse, NY: D. Mason & Co. 1885.

Watson, Winslow C. *The Military and Civil History of the County of Essex, New York*. Albany, N.Y: J. Munsell. 1869.

Williams, Jacqueline. Food on the Oregon Trail. *Oregon-California Trails Association Overland Journal* - Volume 11, No. 2 – 1993.

NOTES

[1] H.P. Smith, History of Essex County, p. 97.

[2] Ibid. p. 98.

[3] Ibid. p. 109.

[4] Ibid. p. 133.

[5] Ibid. p. 133.

[6] Issue number 37 of *The Antiquarian*, Clinton County Historical Association, 1992.

[7] H.P. Smith, History of Essex County, p. 155.

[8] Ibid. p. 157.

[9] Ibid. p. 158.

[10] Willsborough Town Record, 1788. Willsboro Heritage Society Museum, Willsboro, New York.

[11] H.P. Smith, History of Essex County. p. 274.

[12] Ibid. p. 445.

[13] Ibid. p. 446.

[14] Ibid. p. 445.

[15] Ibid. p. 448.

[16] Ibid. p. 441.

[17] Ibid. p. 273.

[18] Census of 1800. Retrieved from Ancestry on July 1, 2018.

[19] H.P. Smith, History of Essex County, p. 157.

[20] Ibid. p.274

[21] Town of Willsborough Records, 1801. Willsboro Heritage Society Museum, Willsboro, New York.

[22] Town of Willsborough Records, 1802. Willsboro Heritage Society Museum, Willsboro, New York.

[23] Town of Willsborough Records, 1802. Willsboro Heritage Society Museum, Willsboro, New York.

[24] Town of Canaan, State of Connecticut Historic Plaque.

[25] Early Historical Highlights of the Town of Canaan, by town historian Elizabeth Clark, Town of Canaan. Retrieved from Web Townhall on July 1, 2018.

[26] Early Historical Highlights of the Town of Canaan, by town historian Elizabeth Clark, Town of Canaan. Retrieved from Web Townhall on July 1, 2018.

[27] Deed research by H. Erwin Hale for clear title to acquire Scragwood, 1950.

[28] Clark Family Tree, Clark Collection. New York State Library, Albany, NY.

[29] Clark Family Tree, Clark Collection. New York State Library, Albany, NY.

[30] Deed between Zacheus Wileas of New Marlborough in the County of Berkshire and Commonwealth of Massachusetts Bay Yeoman and George Clark of New Marlborough aforesaid bloomer June 19, 1799.

[31] Deed research by H. Erwin Hale for clear title to acquire Scragwood, 1950. Clark Collection.New York State Library, Albany, NY.

[32] The Story of an Old Home in Willsboro, New York, Alice Higby Downes, 1974, undated, p. 4.

[33] Ibid. p. 5.

[34] Teaching with Documents: Launching the U.S. Navy, National Archives and Records Administration, Center for Legislative Archives, Records of the U.S. Senate, Record Group 46.

[35] The Military and Civil History of the County of Essex, New York, Winslow C. Watson, Albany, N.Y: J. Munsell, State Street, 1869. p. 438.

[36] Ibid. p. 438.

[37] Ibid. p. 438.

[38] Retrieved from Vermont Archaeology on July 1, 2018.

[39] The Military and Civil History of the County of Essex, New York, Winslow C. Watson, Albany, N.Y: J. Munsell, State Street, 1869. p. 438.

[40] Food on the Oregon Trail, Jacqueline Williams, Oregon-California Trails Association Overland Journal - Volume 11, No. 2 – 1993, [Printed with Permission of Jacqueline Williams 2007].

[41] Retrieved from Vermont History on January 18, 2018.

[42] Greenwood Road (2018, April 10). Retrieved on July 1, 2018 from FamilySearch Wiki.

[43] Turnpikes and Toll Roads in Nineteenth-Century America. Daniel B. Klein, Santa Clara University and John Majewski, University of California – Santa Barbara.

[44] Two Centuries of Ferry Boating, Ralph Nading Hill, Lake Champlain Transportation Company, 1972.

[45] H.P. Smith History of Essex County, p. 160.

[46] "History of Vergennes." Retrieved from Town of Vergennes's website on May 15, 2018.

[47] "Sail Ferry," Retrieved from Tricoastal on March 8, 2018.

[48] Federal Census Record of 1800. Retrieved from Ancestry on May 9, 2018.

[49] 1803 Willsborough Town Records. Willsboro Heritage Society Museum, Willsboro, New York.

[50] Story of Three Towns, Morris F. Glenn, 1977, p. 265.

[51] The Manufacture of Charcoal Iron at Centre Furnace. Centre Furnace Historical Society, 2013.

[52] Old Pattern Admiralty Long Shanked Anchor, North Head, Sydney. Conservation Management Plan. Heritage Office, NSW Australia, April 2000.

[53] Private interview with Ron Bruno, Willsboro Town Historian on July 5, 2016.

[54] Retrieved from New York State, Department of Environmental Conservation's website on July 1, 2018.

[55] Retrieved from Trout Unlimited Stream Explorers on July 1, 2018.

[56] Retrieved from Historic Williamsburg on February 14, 2018.

[57] Levins, Sandy. *A Return to the 18th Century, The Herb Garden.* Retrieved from Then and Now, Historic Camden.

[58] Retrieved from Historic Williamsburg on February 14, 2018.

[59] Retrieved from Historic Williamsburg on February 14, 2018.

[60] Retrieved from Historic Williamsburg on February 14, 2018.

[61] Retrieved from Historic Williamsburg on February 14, 2018.

[62] Michael Olmert, Smokehouse, Foursquare and Solid, Colonial Williamsburg Journal, Winter 2004-2005.

[63] Town of Willsborough Records, 1804. Willsboro Heritage Society Museum, Willsboro, New York.

[64] Town of Willsborough Records, 1804. Willsboro Heritage Society Museum, Willsboro, New York.

[65] Jay's Treaty: The Transformation of Lake Champlain Commerce, H. Nicholas Muller III, Vermont History, The Proceedings of the Vermont Historical Society, Winter/Spring 2012, pp. 33-35.

[66] Willsboro Town Records, 1805. Willsboro Heritage Society Museum, Willsboro, New York.

[67] Private interview with Ron Bruno, Willsboro Town Historian on July 5, 2016.

[68] The Story of Vermont: A Natural and Cultural History, Christopher McGrory Klyza and Stephen C. Trombulak, University Press of New England, Jan. 6, 2015.

[69] Ibid. p. 66.

[70] H.P. Smith, History of Essex County, p. 174.

[71] Ibid. p 274.

[72] Town of Willsborough Records of 1805. Willsboro Heritage Society Museum, Willsboro, New York.

[73] Town of Willsborough Records of 1805. Willsboro Heritage Society Museum, Willsboro, New York.

[74] Private interview with Ron Bruno, Willsboro Town Historian, on July 5, 2016.

[75] Private Interview with Ron Bruno, Willsboro Town Historian, on July 5, 2016.

[76] Town of Willsborough Records, 1807. Willsboro Heritage Society Museum, Willsboro, New York.

[77] Town of Willsborough Records, 1807. Willsboro Heritage Society Museum, Willsboro, New York.

[78] H.P. Smith, History of Essex County, p. 174.

[79] Lake To Locks Passage, New York's Great Northern Journey.

[80] Town of Willsborough Records, 1807. Willsboro Heritage Society Museum, Willsboro, New York.

[81] Clark Family Tree, Clark Collection. New York State Library, Albany, NY.

[82] Phineas Jacquays is spelled Phinchas Jacquays in the US Census of 1820. Retrieved from Ancestry.com on July 1, 2018.

[83] Hannah does not appear in the 1820 census and the female listed in Phineas' household matches the age group of Lydia.

INDEX

Addison, 37, 43
Adsits, 10
Aiken Abraham, 9, 92, 98
Alanson, 17, 55, 59, 60
Albany, 7, 8, 31, 32, 33, 35, 110, 113
Allen. See Allen Ebenezer
Allen Ebenezer, 8
Allen Ethan, 8
Arnold, 8, See Arnold Benedict
Arnold Benedict, 7, 8
Ashley Falls, 28, 29, 31, 32
Atlantic, 93, 94
Bacon Daniel, 10
Barber's Point, 37
Barney Samuel, 10
Basin Harbor, 43
Bennington, 8, 33, 34, 35
Bennington, Vermont, 8
Berkshire Mountains, 13
Berkshires, 31, 50, 55
blockhouse, 11, 95
books, 4
Boquet. See Boquet River
Boquet river, 9, 66
Boquet River, 1, 7, 18, 52, 53, 65, 70, 82
Bridport, 42
British Navy, 93
Brookfield, 99
Brooklyn, 3, 4
Brown Samuel, 9, 60
Burgoyne, 8
Calvin, 91, 103
Calvin Bethewel, 91

Canaan, 13, 14, 15, 16, 17, 19, 21, 23, 28, 32, 36, 37, 46, 53, 57, 59, 60, 64, 70, 73, 76, 84, 86, 96, 112
Canada, 8, 93
Champlain Valley, 8, 93, 96
Charles, 18, 19, 37, 43, 44, 45, 46, 47, 48, 49, 50, 51, 52, 53, 65, 66
Charlotte, 37, 41, 43, 44, 45, 46, 48
Charlotte Harbor, 45
Chesterfield, 9, 10, 99
Chimney Point, 37
Chloe, 17, 55, 56, 57, 58, 59, 60, 61, 62, 84, 86
Clark, 1, 3, 4, 13, 14, 17, 19, 20, 45, 46, 47, 55, 60, 65, 112, 116
Clark family. *See* Clark
Clarks. *See* Clark, *See* Clark
Clinton County, 10, 11, 109, 111
Connecticut, 13, 15, 112
Cooley Levi, 9, 60
Crown Point, 95
Cuyler Stephen, 9, 98
Daniel, 9, 10, 11, 17, 18, 19, 65, 66
Daniel Ross, 9, 10, 11, 17, 18, 19, 65, 66
Elizabethtown, 95, 98
England, 33, 35, 93, 94, 109, 115

121

Essex, 10, 11, 95, 98, 109, 110, 111, 113, 115, 116

Essex County, 10, 11, 95, 98, 109, 111, 115, 116

Essex County Court of Common Pleas, 10

Essex County Turnpike Company, 98

Ferrisburgh, 44, 45

Fisher Asa, 10

Fort Ann, 17, 18, 55, 65

Fort Edward, 71

Fort St. Frederic, 37

Free Commoners, 98

French and Indian War, 7

George, 5, 13, 14, 15, 16, 18, 19, 21, 22, 23, 24, 28, 29, 30, 31, 32, 33, 34, 35, 36, 37, 38, 41, 42, 43, 46, 47, 48, 49, 50, 51, 53, 54, 55, 56, 57, 58, 59, 60, 61, 62, 63, 64, 65, 66, 67, 68, 69, 70, 71, 73, 74, 75, 76, 77, 78, 79, 81, 82, 83, 84, 85, 86, 87,88, 89, 91, 92, 93, 94, 95, 96, 97, 98, 99, 101, 112

Gilliland

William, 7, 8, 9, 11, 17

Great Barrington, 28, 31

Great Northern Turnpike, 98

Greenwood Road, 31, 32, 113

Grog Harbor, 43, 98

Hannah, 14, 102, 107, 116

Higby, 17, 18, 55, 57, 60, 65, 101, 109, 113

Higby Levi, 16, 18, 20, 65, 84, 98, 101

Hoffnagel John and Melchor, 9

Hoffnagel Melchor, 9

Housatonic, 13, 16, 29, 31, 32

Hudson River, 71

iron works, 14, 15, 16, 19

Jakeways, 14, 102

Jay Treaty, 93

John Hoffnagle, 9

Kane Charles, 18, 65, 66

Keene, 10

Lake Champlain, 1, 3, 7, 17, 18, 41, 43, 45, 52, 71, 82, 92, 93, 109, 113, 115

Lake George, 98

Levi, 9, 16, 18, 19, 20, 53, 54, 55, 56, 59, 60, 65, 66, 67, 68, 69, 70, 71, 73, 78, 84, 91, 92, 93, 94, 95, 98, 101

Levi, Jr, 55

Lewis, 95, *See* Clark

Ligonier Point, 2

Ligonier Way, 1

Litchfield County, 13

Lucy Mira, 88, 91

Lydia, 5, 14, 15, 19, 21, 22, 23, 25, 28, 29, 30, 31, 32, 33, 34, 35, 36, 38, 41, 42, 43, 44, 45, 46, 47, 49, 51, 53, 54, 55, 56, 57, 58, 59, 60, 61, 64, 73, 74, 75, 76, 77, 79, 81, 83, 84, 85, 86,

87, 88, 91, 95, 96, 97, 101
Lydia Amanda, 97
Lynde Jonathan, 9, 10, 98
Manchester, 35, 36
Massachusetts, 13, 15, 17, 19, 28, 112
McCrea, 70
McNeil, 11, 37, 43, 44, 45, 46, 47, 53
McNeil Charles, 53
Milltown, 7, 8, 18
Montresor Patent, 10, 18
Morhous John, 9, 10, 97
Nash Truman, 10
Naval Act, 17
Navy, 17, 18, 66, 68, 70, 101
New England, 35
New Marlborough, 15, 16, 19, 21, 22, 23, 57, 59, 62, 64, 70, 73, 112
New York, 3, 4, 1, 4, 5, 7, 9, 14, 17, 18, 31, 34, 37, 38, 45, 47, 50, 52, 53, 109, 110, 113, 114, 116
New York City, 7, 9
New York, 7

Noble Belden, 92, 98
North Ferrisburgh, 44
Orrin, 1, 5, 15, 21, 28, 29, 31, 38, 53, 55, 57, 59, 77, 82, 97
Orrin Clark, 1
Orrin, 1

Orwell, 41
Otter Creek, 43

Peru, 9
Phineas, 14, 102, 107, 116
Pittsfield, 28, 31, 32, 33
Pleasant Valley, 95
Polly, 15, 21, 28, 29, 31, 38, 53, 54, 55, 57, 58, 59, 75, 76, 82, 97
Poor Fund, 103
Port Henry, 37, 98
potash, 43, 94
Rensselaer Turnpike, 33
Revolution, 11
Revolutionary War, 34, 50
Reynolds James, 92
Richelieu River, 71
Rogers Platt, 9, 19
sail ferry, 11, 46, 47, 53
Sally, 16, 21, 25, 28, 29, 31, 38, 42, 48, 51, 54, 55, 57, 58, 60, 74, 75, 76, 78, 82, 84
Scragwood, 2, 3, 112
Sheldon Daniel, 9
Sheldon Joseph, 98
Shoreham, 41, 42
Sloop Island, 50
Solomon. *See* Clark
Split R. ock Mountain, 9
Split Rock Mountain, 37, 43, 51
St. Lawrence River, 71
Stafford
Thomas, 92

Stillwater, 7, 14
Stockbridge, 28, 31, 32
Stower Thomas, 98, 99
Stroud William, 10
Taylor Stephen, 9, 10

The Point. See
    Willsborough Point
Throop, 17, 18, 65, 73, 84,
    94, 98, 101
Town of Willsborough. See
    Willsboro
U.S. Navy, 66, 113
United States, 3, 16, 93
Vergennes, 43
Vermont, 34, 37, 45, 109,
    113, 115
War of Independence, 18
Wells, 36
West Troy, 70, 71, 101
Westport, 37
Whitehall, 71

Wileas Zacheus, 15, 112
William, 7, 10, 11, 17
Williamstown, 33
Willsboro
Willsborough, 1, 4, 5, 109,
113, 114, 115, 116

Willsboro Point, 1
Willsborough, 9, 10, 11,
    17, 18, 19, 20, 22, 35, 36,
    37, 44, 45, 48, 51, 52, 53,
    54, 55, 58, 60, 65, 68, 70,
    71, 82, 84, 89, 91, 95, 96,
    97, 99, 101, 102, 111,
    112, 114, 115, 116
Willsborough Point, 10

ABOUT THE AUTHOR

For Darcey Hale, history has been a passion since, as a ten-year-old, she was introduced to the world of antiquity while residing temporarily among the Mayan ruins of Chichen Itza and Uxmal in Yucatan. This experience was the catalyst for her ongoing quest to learn more about those who had lived in a time gone by.

While earning her B.A. in American Cultural History at Vassar College her approach to history became more defined as she discovered that her true interest was in the people, the world in which they lived, and how their lives played out in a variety of settings. She went on to earn an M.A. in Education from Villanova University and had a long career as a teacher and a school head. With her retirement came the opportunity of a lifetime.

She moved to Willsboro, New York and became the guardian of the treasures that the Clark family had left behind. Through their legacy she has lived their lives and now, in her first book, shares the story of the Clark family, as it so vividly portrays nineteenth century life in New York's Champlain Valley.

HALE HISTORICAL RESEARCH FOUNDATION

The year 2013 clearly delineated the historic importance of the Clark family, their former property and the legacy they left for the future. The property was designated the Ligonier Point National Historic District, the Garden Club of America recognized the importance of the restoration of the Colonial Revival Scragwood garden and this project was recorded in the Smithsonian Archives of American Gardens, Adirondack Architectural Heritage honored the restoration and preservation of Scragwood, and the Erwin and Alma Hale Historic Research Foundation (a not-for-profit 501(c)(3)) organization was chartered as an education corporation by the New York State Board of Regents.

A Board of Directors comprised of historians, museum curators, and family and community members was appointed to guide and oversee the Foundation. Its mission is to recognize and support the cultural heritage of the State of New York and, in particular, Willsborough and the Champlain Valley, and to share and interpret the dimensions of the agricultural, industrial, maritime, economic, social and cultural lives of their inhabitants in the nineteenth century in order to enhance a deeper understanding and appreciation of its history and to promote scholarly research.

The Board of Directors worked tirelessly to find a location in the Champlain Valley that would house the Clark Collection and make it accessible to the general public. However, its enormity made this impossible. In the spring of 2017, the New York State Librarian expressed an interest in the paper portion of the Collection, and subsequently offered to accept this in its entirety. The future of the textile and clothing portion of the Clark Collection is still uncertain although the New York State Museum has expressed considerable interest in accepting all, or a portion, of these items.

The work of the Hale Historical Research Foundation Board is nearing completion. When the Clark Collection in its entirety has been transferred to a permanent home the Foundation will be dissolved.

A Brooklyn-based, independent publisher with a focus on revolutionary ideas for culture, education, and human development.

For a listing of books published by TBR Books, visit our website at:

tbr-books.com